DON'T PUSH ME

Ewan McGregor

There's only so much one woman can take…

For Tricia

1

Kat Matthews had just finished another hellish shift at the bank where she worked.

She was looking forward to getting home. Not that she had much to look forward to when she got there, though the bottle of rosé chilling in the fridge would surely improve her mood.

Kat took the lift down to the underground car park; it was three flights of stairs, after all. She was the only one in the tiny lift, which was a blessing on a day like today. The last thing she needed right now was having to make small talk with one of her inane colleagues.

Kat had an uneasy feeling as she slowly descended. She couldn't quite put her finger on it. The rickety lift was unreliable at the best of times, and if it broke down now, it would cap the day off perfectly.

The lift shuddered as it reached the ground floor. The doors didn't open. Stuck in a lift with no one around. Surely her luck couldn't be that lousy? Thankfully, after a few tense moments and a few choice words, the doors ceded and slowly creaked apart.

Kat stepped out into the bank's car park, where the uneasy feeling didn't subside. If anything it was worse. There was always something creepy about underground car parks, especially when there was not another soul around. To make matters worse, the already dim lighting had started to annoyingly flicker on and off. The bank made millions every quarter but couldn't even replace a few dodgy bulbs? It summed them up really.

Kat had a horrible feeling that someone was lurking there. Or, at the very least, she was being watched. Her heart rate had increased and her stomach was churning. Beads of sweat had formed on her forehead and upper lip. The poorly lit car park had CCTV, and she knew a security guard was stationed near the exit, but that didn't reassure her. It just meant they would be able to watch her being bludgeoned to death at a later date. She moved slowly towards the spot where she had parked her car that morning.

Someone was watching her. She could sense it. She could feel it. Her heart was going like the clappers—

Suddenly, there was a loud bang. Kat almost jumped out of her skin. Someone scuttled away – just out of her eyeline.

She froze, then wiped the sweat from her head and lip with the back of her hand.

As she turned to where the noise had come from she saw, to her relief, a small fox. It must have knocked over one of the bins in its search for scraps.

Kat was a nervous wreck; her heart was racing and she was sweating more than any normal human should. She reached into her bag and fumbled for her keys, then quickly moved to the car.

That's when she noticed the glass glistening on the ground.

Kat moved to assess the damage. Someone had put a half brick through her driver's-side window, and there was a huge score down the driver's door.

What a shitty thing to do.

Kat burst into tears. It was frustration more than anything. She would have to speak to the security guard and see if he had seen anything or if the CCTV had picked it up. Then it was the hassle of dealing with the damage and the insurance. There went her no-claims bonus.

Just as Kat was beginning to clear up the glass on the front seat, a message came through on her mobile. She fished it out of her pocket.

Watch you don't cut yourself on the glass. Safe journey home
xxx

It was them.
Why could they not leave her alone?

2

Kat lived alone in a nice quaint flat in Glasgow's West End. Well, not completely alone – her cat, Kiddles, kept her company.

The flat was a couple of minutes' walk to the underground station at Kelvinbridge. Kat had stayed there since she left her mum's twenty odd years ago and had never envisaged moving. It was a lovely quiet area, plus it was handy for her morning commute to work in the city centre. However, she had to admit that, more often than not these days, she was being lazy and taking the car to work. No wonder she had stopped losing weight again.

Kat tried to park the damaged car outside her flat but someone had stolen her space. Again. The lovely new silver Mercedes had taken her space on numerous occasions now, even though it was clearly marked. Why was she such a pushover? There was a young guy wearing a flash suit exiting the car parked in Kat's designated space.

'Excuse me. Is there any chance of moving your car? You're in my space.' Kat wouldn't normally have said anything; she would just have found another space, no doubt a good distance from her flat. Today though, she felt the need to say something.

'Fuck off,' the young man replied. He laughed at Kat and walked on without a care in the world.

Kat did what she always did. She drove on and parked further down the street, internally scolding herself for letting people walk all over her. She locked the door and assessed the patch-up job she had carried out on the beaten-up Mini. The cardboard and bin bag would have to do for now. There was nothing of value in the car so, hopefully, it would be left alone overnight. She would get it repaired in the morning – no doubt at significant cost.

The bottle of wine was at the forefront of Kat's mind – she needed a drink to settle her nerves. She needed a drink to try to forget about everything.

As she started to walk towards her flat, the heavens opened and the rain came down in sheets. Kat didn't even have an umbrella with her. Great.

Kat's hair was matted to her head as she hurriedly opened the door to get in out of the rain. She was immediately greeted by her faithful companion Kiddles, who nuzzled into her leg. She could always rely on the cat to cheer her up. He would never let her down.

'What would I do without you, Kiddles?' Kat said, stroking the cat.

Kat didn't bother to take off her shoes or jacket, even though she was soaking wet. She lumbered over the ever growing pile of mail on the floor – no doubt more bills her ex-husband had racked up – and moved to the fridge, then poured herself a healthy glass of wine. Kat knocked back a good part of the glass in one go, and then struggled out of her wet clothes before decamping to the couch, bottle in hand. Kiddles followed and curled up next to her. She didn't bother turning the television on. Sitting in the tranquillity of the flat, listening to the rain hammering down outside, her mind was working overtime, turning things over and over. How had it come to this?

Kat used to love working at the bank – that's what made it all the more infuriating. She even enjoyed working weekends when overtime was being offered. Now, she tried to spend as little time there as possible without putting her job in jeopardy. Most of her friends had left or retired over the past few years, which meant she had no support or anyone to confide in. Now she woke up with dread every morning at the thought of going into the office. It was making her unwell, and she knew she was drinking far too much. It was as if she was trying to blank it all out. Kid herself on that she wasn't allowing this to happen.

Bullying. That's what it was – plain and simple. There were two main culprits, Rachel and Kirsty, but lots of others in the office were complicit. They had made her life a misery for around six months now, which was far too long in anyone's book. Kat's confidence had been completely destroyed.

Kat had worked at the bank for the best part of two decades without any problems whatsoever, but then Rachel had started working there and shortly afterwards the bullying had begun. She had no idea what she had said or done to have upset Rachel so much; she had no clue why she, and no one else, was being picked on.

She had tried to nip it in the bud right at the beginning – she had gone to see her manager and told him what was going on. A problem shared is a problem halved, is that not what they say? Not when you had a manager like Tony. To say he was inept would be to do a huge disservice to inept people. He was absolutely bloody hopeless, and it was around this time that things took a turn for the worse.

The bullying had increased worryingly since her chat with management. She felt sure her 'private' conversation with Tony had been anything but. That's also when the text messages had started. Kat had wondered how they had got hold of her mobile number, but she had a feeling – in fact she was absolutely one hundred per cent certain – that Tony had something to do with it.

Now they were targeting her car as well. Where would it stop?

The rosé wine had disappeared rapidly. Kat hadn't even registered the taste. She poured herself another generous measure from the bottle positioned handily at her feet and tried to calm down. Tried to think through the options which were available to her. She could, and probably should, take her concerns further up the ladder to higher management or HR, but she was worried about what might happen and she hated making a fuss. She should show them the text messages – show them her damaged car. There was plenty of evidence. She should also complain about Tony and the way he had dealt with her complaint. Nobody likes a grass though, do they?

She could go off on the sick, but why should she stop working because of silly young girls? And that's just what they were. Girls. They were young enough to be her daughter. Plus, going off on the sick would just delay the problem; it wouldn't make it go away. It was just pushing it further down the road. Or she could grow a set and actually sort the bullies out once and for all. A smile crossed her lips. How good would that be? She knew deep down though that it wouldn't happen – she didn't have it in her. It wasn't in her make-up but it was nice to dream about it.

Kat's head was thumping now. She grabbed a couple of painkillers from the kitchen cupboard and washed them down with yet more wine.

Kat knew things couldn't go on like this. Something had to give.

Something had to change.

3

The fat cow doesn't know what's going to hit her.

Last night it was her banger of a car but that was nothing. Who's she trying to kid anyway? A Mini for someone as fat as that? She must be wedged in tight. A wee brick through the window and a scratch on the paintwork wasn't my finest work, but it sends her a message. Lets her know we're not going away. Keeps her on her toes. She could do with the exercise. It'll be a hassle trying to sort it out, plus it'll hopefully cost her a few quid. Not like she can't afford it.

She should count herself lucky. It might be someone she cares about next.

I could get Jason to batter that son of hers no bother at all. Jason would do it as well – he does anything I want. Daft as a brush but he has his uses and his name carries some weight. Well, his family's name does – people are shit scared of his family, as he keeps on telling anyone stupid enough to listen.

I've heard Fat Kat's mum's not got long left either so I could even put her out of her misery, but then again, I'm not that cruel. Or am I?

I've waited years for the chance to get to the fat bitch and I'm not going to waste the opportunity now.

The first few months I had to tread carefully, but now I'm more liked in work than she ever was and I've got most people turned against her. Tony's the manager, after all, and he's eating out the palm of my hand. Men are so easy to manipulate.

It's going to start for real now.

Thinks she can treat us like that and get away with it? No chance.

She doesn't even know who she's dealing with, that's the best part. She probably thinks it's nothing personal. Little does she know. She'll find out soon enough –

I'm going to make damn sure of that.

Sitting there in her expensive posh flat in the West End while we struggled. How is that fair? Bet she didn't even give it a moment's thought.

Fat bitch has been lucky so far but her luck has well and truly run out. No more playing games and having fun with her; no more kid's stuff – the real pain's going to start now.

I'm going to enjoy every last minute of it.

4

Kat woke with a start. She had fallen asleep on the couch again. She looked at her watch. It showed 3 a.m. How long had she been out?

Her mouth was as dry as a sandpit and her head was still pounding.

She stood and nearly tripped over the two empty wine bottles and wine glass which had been discarded at her feet. At least she knew the reason behind the headache. This had happened far too often lately. Kat had never been a big drinker until the bullying had escalated. She had never really drunk any alcohol at home, bar the odd glass of wine with dinner if she had any friends round. When she used to have friends round. She hadn't seen any of them in months; she just didn't feel like meeting anyone for fear of them finding out how miserable she was. For fear of them finding out she was being bullied. She didn't think she could deal with the embarrassment. She hardly even spoke to them nowadays.

Kat picked the bottles up from the living-room floor and stumbled into the kitchen. That's where the painkillers were. She deposited the bottles in the bin and opened the cupboard, then sank three painkillers with a glass of water – two would not be enough; not after two bottles – and made to go to bed. It was a good job she had the next morning off work. Her hangover was going to be a good one. She could feel it already, plus she had to put her car into the garage and visit her mother at the nursing home.

As she entered her bedroom, Kat noticed her phone lying on the bed. It was illuminated. She had several notifications, which was unusual. She slid her finger across the handset. There was a message from them.

You didn't tell us you were on a dating website? You filthy, desperate cow! xxx

There was a link and, reluctantly, Kat pressed it.

It was as bad as she feared. They had Photoshopped her head onto a younger, thinner, scantily clad woman and signed her up for a dating site. And not one of the fancy ones. Kat felt her head pulsing. Some of the things they had written. Some of the things they had said she was into. Kat didn't understand half of it. Disgusting little witches.

Kat read with horror, bile rising in her stomach. Colour had risen to her cheeks and she felt sick. Why were they targeting her? What had she done to deserve all of this? Why was it only her? It was getting worse.

There were also two notifications from the dating site informing her that she had two new contacts who liked her profile. *I'll bet they did, filthy sods.*

Kat's headache was getting worse the more she read. A mixture of the wine and the sheer anger at these bloody girls who wouldn't leave her alone. They were making her life a misery for no reason whatsoever.

Enough was enough. Something had to be done about this.

Kat hurled the phone across the room, dropped onto her bed and cried herself to sleep.

5

'How are you feeling, Mum?' Kat asked.

She hoped this visit to the nursing home would be pleasant; her hangover couldn't cope with any of her mother's 'episodes' today. Plus, she had a busy morning planned before she had to head for work.

Kat's mother sat in her usual swinging chair, staring out the window. She turned at the sound of Kat's voice.

'Somebody's stole ma teeth,' Maureen Matthews said, opening her mouth wide so Kat could see the lack of dentures.

'Oh, I don't think so, Mum; they've maybe just been misplaced.'

'I'm telling ye, somebody's got them. They probably don't even fit in their mouth. My nice big teeth in somebody's small mouth. It's bloody disgusting.'

Kat tried not to laugh. However, she was going to have to speak to one of the carers. Her mum looked and sounded terrible without her teeth in, and even if somebody hadn't stolen them, they were still missing.

'I'll try and find them,' Kat said. 'Don't worry.'

'Don't worry?' Maureen said. 'That's easy for you to say. It'll be that Irene Jenkins. She's always stealing people's stuff. She's a bloody tea leaf, no two ways about it and she's a proper hussy as well!'

'Now, now – don't be like that.'

Kat's mum had been in the nursing home for over a year now. It had been a struggle getting her a place, and it had been a long few months until she had felt settled and stopped asking to go home. Maureen was eighty-four years old and had lived independently up until last year, but she had mild Alzheimer's, and had good days and bad. Kat didn't know what awaited her every time she visited.

She still couldn't bring herself to put her mum's flat on the market, even though it was lying empty and would fetch a small fortune. There were just too many memories there – plus the views of Kelvingrove Park were stunning. Unfortunately, there was no way her mum would be moving back in.

'What you here for at this time of day anyway, Katherine?' Maureen said. She had become much blunter the older she got – there were no airs and graces about her and she basically told it as it was. Sometimes the consequences were a little awkward or embarrassing, but not it seemed for Maureen.

'I was putting my car into the garage this morning and had a bit of free time before work so thought I would give my dear old mum a visit,' Kat said.

'Aye, well don't make a habit of it. I've got my routines and you're messing that up. *This Morning* starts soon so you'll need to be gone by then. And, less of the "dear old mum" nonsense.'

Kat laughed. 'It's just a fleeting visit.'

'What's happening with you anyhow? Have you gone for the new job yet?'

Kat had confided in her mum a while back that she wasn't happy in her current role at the bank; she didn't think her mum had taken much notice but she was obviously taking in more than Kat gave her credit for. Kat had failed to mention she was unhappy due to being bullied though; she was sure that wouldn't go down well, and the last thing Kat needed was a lecture from her mother about how to stand up for herself.

'No, I've not taken the leap yet,' Kat replied.

'Well, you better get a bloody move on. Time waits for no man or woman – I'll tell ye that for nothing.'

'I know, Mum. I'll get to it soon enough.'

'Aye, you've been saying that for years. Just get a move on or before you know it you'll be as old and dotty as me.' Maureen gave Kat a gumsy smile.

Kat stifled a laugh again. Her mother didn't hold back but she certainly gave good advice. If only she could grab the bull by the horns and try for a promotion. But her confidence had taken a kicking recently and as usual she kept putting it off.

'Have you got everything you need?' Kat asked as she sorted through her mum's clothes.

'Aye, I've got everything I could ever wish for, apart from ma bloody teeth.'

'I'm sure we'll find them soon.'

'Somebody better find them. I can hardly eat anything at the moment apart from soup. The mess I made with my breakfast earlier! You should have seen the poor lassie trying to clean it up. The face she had on her. I told her to stop her mumping and moaning and get on with it; she's getting paid to do it. Anyway, my programme's starting in a minute so…'

Kat could take a hint. 'I'll see you tomorrow, Mum.' She reached over and kissed her.

'Aye, hen, I'll see you soon, but do me a favour, eh? Don't be coming at funny times again. It's messing up my routine.'

6

Kat's morning off work had been productive, even with a bad hangover. She had used some flexi time so she could take her car into the garage. The only downside was that she would have to stay on later one night to make the time back. After her visit to the nursing home, she had checked up on her mother's old flat before getting on the subway and heading to work. She had also contacted the dating site and informed them that someone was playing a cruel prank on her. The supervisor had, thankfully, said she would take the profile down. Hopefully no one she knew had seen the rogue profile yet. At least that was one problem taken care of. Her car would also be ready later that day.

Kat walked slowly to her work. She wasn't in any rush to get there, though that hadn't always been the case.

She had been interested in finance for as long as she could remember. She had always found big business compelling and was forever checking share prices and reading business books. However, her current role was as far removed from what she wanted to be doing as possible. She was in more of an admin or data-entry type role, and although the pay was enough for her modest lifestyle, it wasn't what she aspired to. She had taken the demotion a few years ago when she was in the midst of a messy divorce and her head had been elsewhere, but she had never managed to work her way back up the ladder. Now, there was the bullying to contend with. It was a problem she had never encountered in her life before, even at school. The bullying had resulted in her losing all interest and focus in her work. She had even stopped reading.

*

Kat had been at her desk for nearly an hour and as yet nothing had soured her day. Long may it continue, she thought. However, she was always on edge, waiting on something unpleasant happening. It was a horrible feeling and meant Kat could never allow herself to relax.

An email had come out of the blue informing everyone in the office that Tony would be leaving his current role as manager and they were looking for a replacement. Kat couldn't believe her luck. Maybe they would get someone in who actually knew what they were doing for a change or, at the very least, someone who wouldn't stand for any workplace bullying. How Tony had got the job in the first place was still a complete and utter mystery. Many thought he must have won it in a company raffle. Now, he was moving to a role even higher up in the business. It was no wonder the bank was taking a pounding in the press if this was the calibre of candidate they were actively promoting.

Kat could go for the job; she knew she could do the role standing on her head. It was finding the courage to actually apply that was the stumbling block. Imagine she was the manager and in charge of the two girls who were causing all of her misery? She could solve the problem once and for all.

'Are you going to go for the manager's job, Kat?' Rachel asked, loud enough for most of the office to hear. She was laughing hysterically as if the thought of Kat as manager was the most ridiculous thing she'd ever heard.

And so it begins…

Kat knew where this was going. Unfortunately, she was more than used to it. It had become an everyday occurrence. They were making fun of her.

'I doubt you'd want me as manager,' Kat said, trying to laugh it off as best she could. It was a tactic that had yet to bear fruit. Rachel sneered at her; she hated it when Kat had the audacity to answer back.

'You'd be even worse than the current one!' Kirsty shouted, backing up her horrible friend.

There were a few laughs around the office now. Others were joining in. Tony, for once, had ventured out of his office and stood sniggering like a little schoolboy. Kat wondered what it would take for him to intervene.

'The team lunches would be good – buffets every day!' someone shouted.

They were making fun of Kat's weight. It was an easy joke to make – an easy and tired joke. Something original would be nice.

'Imagine Big Kat telling you you're not getting the bonus.' Another woman laughed. Big Kat. Kat detested being called that.

This happened far too often. It usually started with Kat trying to laugh it off, trying to show they weren't bothering her. It normally ended with her leaving the office and locking herself in the bathroom for a few minutes, either crying or scolding herself for letting them get to her yet again. Kat remembered the old saying 'sticks and stones may break my bones but words will never hurt me'. What a load of old nonsense that was.

She was sick and tired of being laughed at, sick of the snide remarks, the teasing and the mental abuse. She shouldn't have to put up with this. Not at her age. Not at her work.

There wasn't anything she could do though. It had gone on for too long, and Tony had done absolutely nothing to stop it. It was just so frustrating. She was forced to grin and bear it and then drink to excess at night to try to forget about it all.

Kat was fifty-two years old for God's sake – how could she be letting this go on? Bullied at her age? It made her blood boil.

Kat tried to suppress the tears; she didn't want to cry in front of them. She wouldn't give them the satisfaction. She moved off towards the toilets.

She was relieved to get to the relative safety of the toilet cubicle. She locked the door, wiped the seat with toilet paper and sat down, then put her head in her hands and sobbed quietly. Kat knew it was a sorry state to get into. She knew she shouldn't be letting them get to her like this. She just needed to get away from them all, even just for a minute or two. Regain her composure then go out and face them.

Kat took some deep breaths and tried to get herself back on an even keel. She scolded herself internally. She really had to come up with a plan of action. This couldn't go on much longer. There was only so much she could take.

After a few moments, Kat could sense that someone else was in the toilet. She stood up and listened. They were not here to use the facilities. She could hear laughing.

Could they not leave her alone even in here?

Kat composed herself and was ready to go back out and face them. She would confront whoever was laughing on the other side of the door. Tell them enough was enough. Tell them to grow up and act their age. They were all adults, after all.

She moved to leave the toilet cubicle. The door wouldn't budge. She fiddled with the lock, but it was jammed shut. She couldn't get out – she was trapped.

The laughing was louder now. Someone had managed to lock her in the cubicle from the outside.

Kat couldn't get out; she couldn't breathe. Oh God, the walls were closing in.

'Who's out there? Can you let me out?' Kat was panicking now.

The laughing was louder still.

'Help!' Kat pleaded, desperately trying to force the lock open.

'Hopefully someone comes to the rescue soon!' the cackling voice said. It sounded like Rachel – it had to be her.

Then the lights went out. She had locked her in the small cubicle, turned off the lights… and left her there.

Kat was trapped in the pitch-black toilet cubicle. She couldn't move. She was struggling to get a breath.

Then she collapsed to the floor.

7

Kat woke up and immediately knew something was amiss. She wasn't in her own bed. She wasn't sprawled on her couch either. Her head was absolutely banging and this time it had nothing to do with alcohol. She could hear some sort of beeping and compressing of machines. As her eyes slowly focused, she realised to her horror that she was in a hospital ward. All sorts of wires had been affixed to her chest and finger. She was hooked up to noisy machines that were monitoring her vital signs. She brought her hand up to her head and touched what felt, worryingly, like stitches.

'Ah, you're awake,' a nurse said. 'I'll go and fetch Dr Andrade.'

Dr Andrade was obviously very busy, as a considerable period of time passed before he appeared, smiling, at Kat's bedside, holding a clipboard.

'Good morning, Mrs Matthews. Good to see you back with us,' he said, smiling.

'It's Miss Matthews actually.' Kat didn't mean to come across tetchy but that's how it sounded. 'Mrs' brought back painful memories of her failed marriage.

'Sorry about that. Miss Matthews, how are you feeling?'

'I'm a little confused, to be honest. What's happening?'

'We're putting it down to a panic attack,' the young doctor said matter-of-factly.

'A panic attack? I've never had anything like that before,' Kat said.

'These things can and do come out of the blue,' Dr Andrade said, taking a seat beside Kat's bed.

Her head was throbbing; she couldn't take all of this in. A panic attack? She suddenly remembered being stuck in the toilet cubicle at work. The horrible laughing. The darkness.

'It could be a number of things. Maybe you're under a bit of extra stress or it could be something else entirely that has triggered it. The main thing, though, is that you're okay,' the doctor continued, placing his hand on Kat's.

Kat knew exactly what had triggered it.

'My head's really sore,' Kat said, bringing her hand to the stitches again.

'Yes, it will be. I'm afraid you must have given it an almighty whack when you fell. Thankfully, you only needed a couple of small stitches. You should count yourself lucky. I'll fetch you some painkillers. They should do the trick.'

'I don't need to stay in here, do I?' Kat asked. A long hospital stay was the last thing she needed.

'No, no, once you're up and ready and we've given you the once-over, you can be on your way. There should be no lasting damage and there's ways of coping with these attacks,' the doctor said. He was smiling, trying to reassure Kat. It wasn't working.

'Will they come back then?'

'Hopefully this was a one-off.'

'Hopefully,' Kat said.

These silly girls were now causing her to have panic attacks? Were they not going to be happy until they'd caused her death? This had gone way too far.

Enough was enough – it had to stop.

8

Kat left the hospital still feeling very fragile. She couldn't quite believe what had happened to her. What she had allowed to happen. She couldn't believe that her work hadn't called Paul and let him know his mother was in hospital. They hadn't informed anyone by the looks of it, and Kat was left to deal with everything herself. She'd never felt so alone. They hadn't even sent a first aider along with her, even though the bank's own health and safety protocols required them to do so. Tony really was playing at being a manager. He was worse than useless.

The headache still hadn't shifted as Kat took a taxi the short ride home – if anything it was worse.

Kat's neighbour, Mrs Paterson, was loitering outside her flat. She was a nice old lady but a terrible gossip; she was like a one-woman neighbourhood watch. Not much got past her and she loved knowing everyone's business. Kat could really be doing without this today.

'Kat, why are you in a taxi? Where's that lovely car of yours?' Mrs Paterson fired her question machine gun at her. Kat was barely out of the cab and her car could never have been described as lovely.

'Hi, Mrs Paterson. The car's in the garage getting fixed.' This wasn't what Kat needed – a grilling from her elderly neighbour. She just wanted to get into the flat.

'Oh yes, I noticed last night. How did your window get smashed? Whoever would do such a terrible thing?'

'Just a little vandal, I'm afraid. It's nothing to worry about; it'll all be sorted today.'

'And that blasted car taking your space again!' Mrs Paterson went on. 'Why are you not at work?' She was on top form today.

'I've got a wee holiday today.' Kat couldn't bring herself to tell the truth about the panic attack and hospital stay. It would elicit many more questions. Hopefully, Mrs Paterson wouldn't notice the small band of stitches on her head.

'Do you want to come in for a cuppa?'

'Thanks for the offer – maybe another time, Mrs Paterson.'

'Anytime, Kat – you know my door's always open… if you need a wee chat or for anything – anything at all,' Mrs Paterson said. She meant it as well.

Kat thanked her elderly neighbour again whilst backing away and opening the door to her flat.

She didn't need a chat and a cup of tea with Mrs Paterson. All she needed now was a glass of wine and her bed. In that order.

9

It worked out even better than I could have expected.

The fat cow did her usual, sloping off to the toilet for a good greet. She must think we don't know she goes in there to get away from us. It happens most days.

I followed her in with two plans. Plan A was to smash her fat face off the wall. Not exactly subtle but it got the point across well enough. She was already hiding inside the cubicle though, so Plan B was put into action. Plan B was to lock her in the toilet. Not the best plan ever but needs must. She should do the sensible thing and just quit because I'm not going to stop until her life is ruined. Although, even if she does quit, it won't end – I know where the fat bitch stays.

A panic attack! What a laugh. That wasn't part of the plan, but it turned into an unexpected bonus. Pathetic. I could hear her whimpering and shouting for help; I just turned the light off and started to head out of there. Then I heard her hit the floor. Lucky there's not a big dent in it now. It would've been better if she'd lain in there for longer, but ten minutes later that daft Angie Stevenson came running out saying Fat Kat needed an ambulance. Who knows how she got the door open. The fat cow must've forced it open when she fell. Everyone thought she'd had a heart attack the way Angie was screaming and shouting and flapping her stupid arms about. No such luck. An ambulance for a poxy panic attack. What a waste of taxpayers' money, but that summed her up – she wasted everything she was ever given.

Some people in there pissed me off though. Coming up to me, asking if I'd done anything to Kat in the toilet. I never even admitted it – just smiled at them. There was nothing to prove that I did anything to her, but next thing you know, they're saying I went too far. That we need to stop all of this, that they don't want any part of it. No one asked them to get involved. What do they know anyway? Too far? I'll show them too far. They ain't seen nothing yet.

I'm just getting started.

10

Kat was sat on her couch feeling sorry for herself. She had drunk far too much wine. Coupled with the painkillers she had taken – those the hospital had provided and her own supply – it meant she was slipping in and out of consciousness. She knew she needed to stop drinking as much, but to say she was having a bad week would be an understatement.

She had finally gathered up the ever growing pile of mail on the floor. As she suspected and feared, most of it was bills in her ex-husband's name. Some of them were final reminders. The scumbag was still using her address to run up debt even though he hadn't stayed with Kat for nearly ten years now. It was yet another headache to deal with and yet another reason to hit the bottle. She took another mouthful of wine, but as she tried to place the glass on the coffee table, it slipped from her drunken grasp and smashed on the wooden floor. Things were not going well. In her semi-conscious state, Kat tried to compose herself and clean it up, but she only managed to cut herself on the hand. Blood now mixed in with the glass and rosé wine. What a mess.

Kat made her way into the kitchen to where she kept some plasters in a little first-aid box. She haphazardly slapped a couple on her hand to stem the steady flow of blood and replaced the box next to an array of pills.

Looking at the multitude of drugs in the cupboard, Kat got to thinking. She could just take a load more pills along with the wine, be done with it once and for all, she thought morbidly. She had already taken too many painkillers – a few more and it would all be over. It would be easily done. She'd just drift off into a drunken sleep and never wake up. No one would miss her and the torment in work would be at an end. They couldn't make her cry anymore. No more abusive text messages. No more damaging her things. No more taunts or getting locked in the toilet. No more jibes about her weight, and they wouldn't make her have bloody panic attacks.

Then she thought about her son, Paul. He would miss her. She smiled. Of all the things she had done in life, no one could take away the fact that Paul had turned out great, and that was in no small part down to her. She had brought him up by herself – well, with help from her mum and dad, but no help from his no-good father, who hadn't contributed a single penny to his upbringing. He had done a bunk just before Kat gave birth; only reappearing years later when he claimed he wanted to make amends. Kat had been suckered in and nearly lost everything as a result. Nearly even lost her relationship with Paul. The real reason the scumbag had come back was to fleece Kat and then file for a divorce. What a treat he was.

She was proud of her son, and she knew there and then that her fleeting thought of suicide wouldn't come to anything more than that. Who would look after Kiddles if she was gone in any case? She stroked the cat, which had curled up and gone to sleep beside her.

What a state to get into, Kat thought with tears forming. There was no way she should be allowing two silly, immature little girls to lead her to thoughts of ending it all.

She was feeling terrible after her hospital stay and the alcohol really hadn't helped matters. She felt as if she was on the verge of collapse, both physically and mentally. If she carried on drinking the way she had been, she would end up back in hospital, that was for sure. She'd do herself permanent damage. She had always liked the odd glass of wine but would never have been classed as a big drinker. Now she was drinking every night and it was definitely turning into a problem. She resolved to sort herself out. She wouldn't let them win. She wouldn't keep turning to alcohol as a coping mechanism.

Kat turned the television off. She couldn't even remember one programme that had been on; it was just background noise. The living room was a bit of a mess with shards of glass and blood, but it could wait until the morning. She needed to sleep; her bed was calling out to her.

11

Kat's doorbell buzzed.

She was in the middle of sorting out some food for Kiddles and trying to clean up last night's drink-induced mess. Her head was thumping from her fall in the toilet. The large intake of rosé certainly hadn't improved matters.

The doorbell buzzed again.

'I'm coming!' Kat shouted. She still felt exhausted and really shaky. Her hangover was going to be a good one.

She opened the door. Standing on the step was the last person she would have expected. The last person she ever wanted to see.

Rachel.

'What are you doing here?' She was the reason for all of this, yet here she was, bold as brass. Kat couldn't believe her eyes. She felt physically sick at the sight of her. Although, in fairness, last night's wine might have had something to do with that.

'I've come to apologise, Kat,' Rachel said. 'I'm so sorry.'

Kat stood there stunned. How did Rachel even know where she stayed?

'Is this some sort of joke?' Kat said.

'No, Kat, it's no joke,' Rachel said quietly, with her head bowed. 'I feel terrible – I'm so sorry. I can't believe you ended up in hospital.'

Kat should have closed the door and gone back inside. She should have given Rachel a piece of her mind and slammed the door in her face. Instead, she stepped aside and invited her in.

Sitting in her living room, Kat noticed that Rachel was just a slight wee thing. Nothing to be scared of at all. Yet, the uneasy feeling was back. This was completely out of character for Rachel, and Kat couldn't help but think that there was some sort of ulterior motive at play. This could all be some sort of elaborate trick. She wasn't going to offer her a cup of tea and biscuits at any rate.

'I can't believe how I've behaved. I'm here to tell you that you don't need to worry anymore. I've told Kirsty as well – it's gone way too far and that's it. It's done. Nothing will ever happen to you again. I'm so sorry,' Rachel said, whilst surveying the mess of the living room.

Kat couldn't believe her ears. Rachel was either a very good actress or she was genuine. Maybe she really was sorry? There was even the glint of tears in her eyes.

'Why would you lock me in the toilet? Why are you so bloody cruel to me?' Kat asked. She needed some sort of explanation for what she had been put through.

'I... I don't know. It all started out as a bit of a joke and Kirsty kind of led me astray. I know that's no excuse, and I know it's gone way beyond a joke,' Rachel replied. 'I'm so sorry you ended up getting hurt. I just hope you can find it in your heart to forgive me.'

'You smashed my car up. It cost me a fortune—'

'We'll give you the money back, Kat. I'm so sorry.'

'I should've gone to the police. Shown them the damage.'

'I know. I wouldn't blame you if you did. I deserve it, but honestly, Kat, I feel terrible. I'm so, so sorry,' Rachel said again. She couldn't even look Kat in the eye as they spoke. She looked thoroughly ashamed. She looked full of remorse.

'I guess we could start again, let bygones be bygones so to speak,' Kat said. She couldn't believe the words that were coming out her mouth – let bygones be bygones? This was the girl who had, for six months or more, destroyed Kat's life. Yet all she wanted more than anything in the world was for it all to stop. To not wake up every single morning with that feeling of dread in the pit of her stomach. To be able to go to work without fearing what might happen. To look at her phone without fearing what she would see or read. In short, Kat wanted to resume living her life again. She couldn't believe this turn of events; Rachel's visit had taken her completely by surprise.

'That would be great. You'll never know how sorry I am, Kat. I'm so disgusted with myself. I can't believe how I've behaved,' Rachel said.

'It's done now,' Kat replied.

'Well, that's all I came to say. I'll let you get back to it. See you in work. Thanks for being so nice about it,' Rachel said, standing up.

'See you in work.' Kat led her back to the door where Kiddles was standing guard.

'Oh, what a lovely cat,' Rachel said, reaching down to stroke Kiddles. 'I love cats – used to have one myself.'

Rachel petted the cat and then left the flat, leaving Kat thoroughly bemused.

12

Rachel had been true to her word. Kat's next day in work had been just like old. The bullying had stopped. They were never going to be best friends after all that had gone on, but Kat had even exchanged a little hello with Rachel as they passed each other on the way back from the morning break. Not one person had said a cross word to her. They hadn't made fun of her weight or slagged her off for... well, for anything at all. If things continued in this vein then the panic attack might turn out to be the best thing that could ever have happened. A blessing in disguise, so to speak. Kat was allowed to go about her daily business free from taunts, and she felt a great relief, like a huge weight had been lifted from her shoulders. She might even go for that promotion after all if this continued. She had put it off for long enough. It was about time she started thinking about herself and her career prospects again.

Even inept manager Tony was being nice to her. He had called Kat into his office and asked how she was feeling, which had taken her completely by surprise. He hadn't asked her anything at all in months. The last time they had spoken had been when Kat confronted him about Rachel and Kirsty's terrible behaviour and he had been no help whatsoever. Today though, he couldn't have been nicer and seemed to be genuinely concerned about Kat's well-being. He even told her that his brother had suffered from panic attacks in his teens and said he could sympathise.

If every day was like this then Kat would have nothing to worry about at all. Her life could resume again.

At lunchtime, Kat had even made a start trying to deal with her ex-husband using her address to build up yet another mountain of debt. She had made contact with a few of the lenders and tried to explain the situation, telling them that this had happened before and she wasn't averse to the police getting involved if that was the only way the problem could be solved. Kat wasn't sure the customer advisors she had spoken to would solve the matter, but at least it was a start. It was better than burying her head in the sand, pretending that nothing was happening. It made her feel better that she was at least being proactive about the situation.

The only worry Kat had now was the fact she hadn't seen Kiddles before work this morning. She was becoming increasingly worried. It was very unusual. She would have to get Mrs Paterson on the case. She would find him in no time. He had disappeared for a few hours before, but to Kat's mind, he had never missed his morning meal. She was sure that when she went home the cat would have returned. He would be hungry by now.

13

Kat had arranged to meet her son Paul for lunch. He was off for a couple of days from work and needed to pop into the city centre, so he had asked Kat if she was free during her lunch hour. Kat had been delighted to get the call and to accept the invitation. Her luck really was turning.

Kat entered the lovely modern Italian restaurant. It was an ideal location as it was on Bothwell Street, directly opposite the bank. She had never been in before, even though her work had hired the place out last month for a function. Kat had stopped going to any work events since the bullying had started. It was a shame, as her social calendar wasn't exactly jam-packed, and work events used to be one of the rare occasions she had gone for a night out.

Paul was already seated at a table for two by the window as Kat entered. He had a glass of mineral water in front of him.

'Mum, how are you?' Paul said. 'What can I get you to drink?'

'I'm good. I'll just have a mineral water as well,' Kat said.

'You sure I can't tempt you with a wee wine?' Paul replied.

Kat wasn't even tempted today. The urge to drink seemed to be dissipating a little. She needed to distance herself from that particular crutch. There was no need to drink herself into oblivion anymore.

'No, no, mineral water will be fine. Need a clear head for work this afternoon.'

After a few minutes Kat and Paul ordered and sat back, watching the world go by. Glasgow was busy at this time of day and Bothwell Street was packed with workers coming and going on their lunch hour. For once, the rain had stopped and it was turning into a nice afternoon. Kat was always delighted when Paul phoned her to meet up. Their relationship had almost been broken beyond repair around ten years ago when Kat had taken his no-good father back. It had taken months for Paul to even speak to her again, and now when they met up, all conversation about Stephen was strictly off limits. He was like a dark cloud that hung over them even though he was completely out of their lives.

'How's that cat of yours?' Paul asked.

'Kiddles is great – keeps me going.' Kat didn't want to admit she was worried about his current whereabouts.

'And how's work going?'

'I'm just plodding along – you know me.' Kat hadn't confided in Paul about the bullying and now she hoped she would never have to. 'I'm thinking about going for another job in the department. A manager's job,' Kat said.

'You should definitely go for it. You know you could do any job in there; you should be higher up.'

'I know, I know. Anyway, less about boring old me. What about you and Charlotte?'

Paul and Charlotte had been going out for years and had recently bought their first house together. Charlotte was a lovely girl, and Kat was thrilled that their relationship was progressing in the right direction. The couple had been through a few sticky patches over the years but everything seemed to be back on track now.

'That's the reason I suggested lunch, Mum,' Paul said. 'I've got some good news to tell you, but you need to keep it to yourself for a bit. Charlotte's pregnant – you're going to be a granny!'

Kat was in tears before Paul had even finished his sentence – happy tears this time. She was absolutely delighted with the news. She had longed for this more than anything else in the world.

'That's brilliant!' Kat said. She was trying to compose herself and stop attracting attention from the other diners.

'She's just a few weeks so—'

'I'll not say a word,' Kat said, dabbing her eyes with a tissue. 'It's just great news. You don't know how happy this makes me.'

14

Kat kissed Paul goodbye and made her way across the road back to work with a definite spring in her step. The meal had been lovely. The company and the news she had received before the meal had been even better. She was going to be a grandmother. Kat couldn't believe it. She was absolutely delighted. Would it be a little boy? Or a little girl? As long as the baby was healthy, it didn't matter one jot.

Just a couple of days ago Kat had been at her lowest ebb, drinking far too much and contemplating unthinkable actions. It was amazing how things could change so much in a short period of time. How things could be turned completely around. She couldn't stop smiling; she really was on cloud nine.

As Kat entered into the bank's reception area her phone vibrated. She fished it out of her bag. It was her elderly neighbour Mrs Paterson calling. No doubt there was a faulty street light or someone had forgotten to take their bins out on collection day again. Nonetheless, nothing could spoil Kat's mood today after the great news she had just been given. Still smiling, she accepted the call.

'Kat! Oh my goodness… I'm so glad I got you…'

'What's wrong, Mrs Paterson? You'll need to calm down; you've got yourself in a terrible state.'

'Oh, my poor Kat. I can't believe it. Terrible, terrible news.'

'What is it?' Kat was worried now. The smile had gone from her face. This didn't sound like her usual calls from Mrs Paterson.

'It's the cat – it's Kiddles…'

'Mrs Paterson? What's happened?'

'I found him in the garden when I was taking out my recycling—'

'Mrs Paterson?'

'I'm so sorry, Kat. The poor… the poor thing's… dead.'

Kat couldn't breathe again; it was as if her throat had contracted. She steadied herself against the wall before she collapsed. The reception area was busy and a few people stopped and stared.

'Say that again? Mrs Paterson?' Kat was frantic. This couldn't be happening.

'I'm so sorry, Kat – Kiddles is dead.'

15

Kat sat in the uncomfortable old-fashioned chair sipping brandy. It wasn't helping as much as Mrs Paterson had said it would.

Her whole body was trembling. Kat couldn't get her head around what was going on. She couldn't believe it. She didn't want to believe it. She had gone from the euphoria of Paul telling her she was to be a grandmother to the heartache and shock of Mrs Paterson telling her Kiddles was dead.

Kat had driven from work as fast as she could, her head spinning and tears flowing freely. She had hoped and prayed that Mrs Paterson had made some sort of mistake, but she knew that wouldn't be the case.

Poor Kiddles. He had been fine. He'd been at the vet's only a few weeks ago and was in good health. How could this have happened?

Mrs Paterson had kindly invited Kat inside as she did most days. Kat had been that numb she had accepted. She really was all over the place. Only an hour previously, she had been on top of the world – now she had crashed back down to earth with a huge bump. She felt completely at a loss.

'The poor little thing was just lying there. I knew it wasn't looking good right away. I nearly called an ambulance but then you can't phone an ambulance for a cat, can you? Then I thought about phoning a vet but I don't know any vets so I thought I'd phone you. Poor little thing,' Mrs Paterson said as she stroked Kat's hand.

Kat wasn't even properly listening. She was still in shock. She just nodded where she thought it appropriate and tried to focus on her breathing. Tried to stop her body from shaking.

One problem had been solved – the bullying in work – and another had presented itself. Poor Kiddles. Her faithful little companion taken away. She hoped her poor pet hadn't suffered.

'Thanks for phoning me, Mrs Paterson,' Kat said.

'I'm sorry. I knew you'd be at work and it's not ideal telling someone news like this over the phone.'

'No, no, I'm glad you called.'

Kat had finished the brandy and Mrs Paterson immediately refilled her glass. Kat didn't refuse.

'I don't know what we do now?' Mrs Paterson said.

Kat had no idea what her elderly neighbour meant but she realised she was expecting a reply. 'There's not much we can do. No one's going to bring him back…'

'No, I mean with humans, there are certain procedures to go through, autopsy reports and the like, but do we have to contact anyone?'

'I'm not too sure. I don't think so. It's a lot to take in just now.' Kat could feel another headache coming on. Her head was pulsing.

'It must be a terrible shock. You take some more brandy – that'll help you calm down. Will you stay for your tea?' Mrs Paterson asked.

'No, no, I'd better be getting back,' Kat said. 'Thanks for all your help.'

'If you need anything – anything at all, Kat – just give me a chap. You know you're always welcome here, even if you only need a chat or a wee shoulder to cry on.'

'Thanks… but I'll be fine,' Kat said, not believing it.

16

Kat's first day back at work had gone by in a complete blur. She had been in the office in body only. Her mind was most definitely elsewhere.

She had taken two days off after the unexpected and untimely death of her cat. Two days where she had thought about nothing apart from Kiddles. How had he died? Why had he died? Had he suffered? Two days, where instead of feeling happy about Paul and Charlotte's fantastic news as she should, she had moped around the house drinking far too much wine and feeling sorry for herself. She still had come up with no answers as to what had happened or what had caused Kiddles' death. All she knew was that she missed her little companion deeply. The house was far too quiet without him, and the loneliness Kat felt was unreal.

Tony had been surprisingly sympathetic again when she called in to let him know she wouldn't be fit for work. He'd told her to take a few days off and said he would even put it through as compassionate leave. The last thing she should be worrying about was work, he'd said.

The two days leave hadn't helped at all. She was still distraught and still had no clue as to what had actually happened to her beloved pet. Everyone had been great – Paul had been down to visit twice and Mrs Paterson was never away from the door, but Kat hadn't been great company.

They had left her alone at work again today. Rachel had stayed true to her word and Kirsty hadn't come near. At least that was something. If the bullying had resumed, that might have tipped Kat into the abyss.

Kat was glad the day was at an end. Although, the thought that she would now be completely alone when she got home was depressing. That was the reason she had decided to stay on for an hour to make up some of the flexi time she had used to take her car into the garage, though she hadn't managed to catch up on any work. If anything, she was further behind. Kat was at a loss: she didn't want to be in work, but she couldn't face going home.

As she exited the lift and walked through the car park, Kat felt that horrible, uneasy feeling wash over her again. She really had to have a think about parking her car somewhere other than the underground car park. It was no good for her anxiety.

Someone was there. It was no fox this time – she was sure of that.

Kat heard hurried footsteps approaching behind her.

'Kat, how are you?' It was Rachel. She was walking briskly behind her.

'Rachel, you gave me a fright there,' Kat said. 'I'm fine, thanks.'

'I was so sorry to hear about your poor cat.'

'Thanks, it was a terrible shock.'

'I'll bet it was… maybe it was allergic to the little treat I gave it when I came to your flat,' Rachel said, smiling.

It all slowly fell into place. Kat couldn't believe it – Rachel had wormed her way into her home… and poisoned her poor little cat. She had killed Kiddles.

Why? Surely no one could hate her so much as to do such a disgusting, horrible, cowardly thing like that? The girl was a psychopath.

'Why would… How could?' Kat couldn't get her words out. She could feel the colour rushing to her cheeks. How could she have been so stupid as to let her into her home? She had even forgiven her for everything.

'Spit it out, Fat Kat. You think I was actually sorry when I came to your shitty wee flat? I can't believe you let me in! How gullible are you?' Rachel said, as if seeing what Kat was thinking.

'How could you do such a thing?' Kat spluttered. 'My poor cat.'

Rachel stood laughing. Laughing!

She moved closer to Kat.

She had killed Kiddles and now she was actually laughing about it.

'The poor cat didn't have to die…' Rachel said, moving ever closer.

'Why do you hate me so much? What have I ever done to you?' Kat said. She stepped back. There was nowhere for her to go; she was backed right up against her car now.

'It should have been you! Fat Kat and not your little cat. Every time I see you I just want to smash that ugly fat face in,' Rachel said, closer still. They were almost touching now.

'Leave me alone!' Kat shouted, hoping that someone might hear and come to the rescue. Rachel may be a slight little thing but she was threatening her, and the last thing Kat needed right now was a punch in the face.

Unfortunately, the car park remained deserted.

Nobody came.

Rachel moved forward and grabbed Kat by the hair. Kat tried as best she could to shake her off, but Rachel's hand was clamped tight to her head. The two of them struggled back and forth.

'The cat's better off dead! Next time it might be Paul!' Rachel said. She was punching Kat in the stomach with her free hand. She was completely out of control. How did she even know who Paul was?

'Get off me!' Kat shouted. She was boiling with rage now. This evil little girl had killed her cat and now she was threatening her son. Kat swung her hand with all her might and caught Rachel on the side of the head with her fist. She swung again, this time with her other arm. Rachel still wouldn't budge. A third swing and finally her grip loosened. Rachel fell backwards and then—

Silence.

Kat was breathing hard. She put her hand to her head, which was stinging. By sheer luck there was no blood, and her scalp and hair still seemed to be intact. Thankfully, the little witch had avoided ripping the stitches out of Kat's head.

Her attention turned to Rachel. She was lying on the ground, completely still.

Kat leaned in for a closer look. She was cautious though – this could be a trick.

Kat watched Rachel closely.

Oh my God! She wasn't breathing. There was blood trickling from behind her ear!

Kat had done a first-aid course a few years ago; she knew this didn't look good at all. She moved Rachel into the recovery position and checked for a pulse, though she knew it was futile.

Rachel was dead.

17

Kat knew she should have called an ambulance. She could have bundled Rachel into the car and driven her to hospital herself. It was an accident, after all. What if there was still a chance she could be saved?

Kat did neither of these things.

She sat in her car. She could barely move. She tried to get her breathing under control. Tried to make sense of things. She couldn't think straight. Adrenaline was flowing through her body and she felt frozen in the driver's seat. What the hell had just happened? She closed her eyes and tried to calm her breathing. Tried to get on an even keel. Rachel had killed Kiddles. She had threatened Paul. And now she was dead.

After a minute or two Kat opened the driver's door and stepped out. Rachel was still lying lifeless on the ground, blood pooling at her head. It wasn't as if she was going to miraculously jump up and run off, forget any of this had ever happened now, was it?

Kat looked around but still no one had appeared in the dimly lit car park. Why the hell had she chosen to stay on for an extra hour? If someone had appeared in the car park then the decision would have been taken out of her hands. She would have to confess and explain what had happened.

She knew she should be alerting someone.

Anyone.

She should be screaming at the top of her lungs until someone came running to help. The security guard would be positioned at the exit; he would surely hear if she screamed loud enough.

Her mind was racing. The little witch had bullied her mercilessly for months. Every single day she had taunted her and made her a laughing stock. She'd smashed up her car. She had talked her way into her flat and killed her beloved cat. She had just threatened her son. She had just attacked her for no reason. However, Kat never intended to kill her. Kat hadn't hurt anyone her entire life. It was an accident. Self-defence. How unlucky could you be? Killing someone with one punch. It wasn't even a punch. More of a swing of the arm – well, three swings of the arm. What if people thought it wasn't an accident?

How could this be happening?

Decision time.

Kat opened the back door of the Mini. She stood for a moment transfixed by Rachel's lifeless body lying on the ground.

Kat looked left. Looked right. And then bundled Rachel into the back seat of the car.

She used the blanket that had lain in the back for years to hide Rachel's small, limp body and then jumped back out of the car, her breathing laboured.

What on earth was she doing? This was beyond insane.

Kat stood outside the car, steadied by her arm resting on the door. She needed time to think. She needed to breathe. Then she spotted Rachel's bag lying on the ground. She picked it up and threw it in the back as well.

A line had well and truly been crossed.

There was no going back now.

18

Kat closed the Mini's door and stared at the ground adjacent to it. A sizeable bloodstain remained on the concrete. If someone spotted that they would know something untoward had happened and would investigate. The game would be up. There was nothing to clean it up with though, and the longer Kat lingered here, the more chance there was of someone stumbling across this whole sorry mess. There would be no explanation that would make things right.

Kat was panicking again. She tried to slow her breathing. She needed to think rationally. There was a dead girl lying in the back of her car. What she was doing was madness. How could she get rid of the bloodstain? There was a cupboard outside the office which was used by the cleaners. There was bound to be something useful in there. If only she could get to it without anyone seeing her.

Kat lifted her handbrake and moved the car over a touch so it was covering the unforgiving red stain. Then she got out and headed back for the lift.

Kat was sweating. What the hell was she playing at? What if someone saw her going into the cleaning cupboard? What if she came back down and someone had discovered Rachel lying under the cover in her back seat? This was a living nightmare. She needed to have a rethink – it wasn't too late. Go down, take Rachel out of the car and shout for help. Scream to high heaven until someone came. Tell the truth. It was still a viable option. It was the sensible option.

The lift pinged and dragged Kat from her thoughts, opening excruciatingly slowly as usual. If the damn thing broke down now then she was well and truly screwed.

The lift made its agonisingly slow ascent and finally reached the third floor. Kat got out and made her way to the cupboard. She could see that the light was still on in the office, but thankfully no one came out.

She crept forward and opened the cupboard door, scanned the contents of the cupboard and quickly grabbed a bottle of bleach and a scrubbing brush. She hastily closed the door and then set off back towards the lift. She might just get away with this.

'Alright, Kat?' It was Tony, her inept manager. 'I thought you were away home already?' Kat quickly hid the bottle and brush behind her back.

'Forgot my keys. I'd forget my head if it wasn't screwed on.' She laughed. Kat hoped she wasn't as red in the face as she felt. She hoped he wouldn't notice that she was completely drenched in sweat.

'Ah… Alright then, I'll see you in the morning,' Tony said, dismissing Kat and turning to go back into the office. Tony seemed more nervous than Kat was. He was very jumpy and looked a bit dishevelled. His hair was everywhere.

Kat walked briskly to the lift and pressed the button on the wall. She was shaking now; her nerves were shot.

'Come on, come on,' she urged.

The lift must only have taken a matter of seconds to arrive but it felt a lot longer to Kat. She hurriedly got in and hammered the button for the ground floor. She really should have used the stairs so the possibility of the lift breaking down wasn't a factor.

The lift arrived at the ground floor and opened without any complications. Kat stepped out and looked around. Her luck was holding – there still wasn't a soul in the car park. If she had left at her usual finishing time then the place would have been crawling with staff trying to beat each other to the exit.

If she had just finished at her normal time then none of this would ever have happened. It could all have been avoided.

As quickly as she could, Kat made her way to the Mini. She took the handbrake off and pushed the car forward a little to access the bloodstain. Then she poured liberal amounts of bleach on it. It wasn't making much of an impact – if anything, the stain looked bigger.

She grabbed the brush and started scrubbing furiously at the blood and bleach. It had worked a little. The stain could be mistaken for something else now. You didn't immediately think it was blood in any case.

She poured the remaining bleach onto the pinkish stain then got back into the car, making sure to bring the bottle and brush with her. She threw them in the back.

Kat gathered herself together and took a quick peek over her shoulder into the back seat, where the blanket covered Rachel. What the hell had she done?

Kat put the car into gear and drove past the small security booth and out of the car park.

Her life had just changed forever.

19

Kat's mind was spinning as she drove home. What in God's name was she doing? This was crazy.

She could picture everything clearly in her head.

The police slapping handcuffs on her.

The jail cell.

The court case.

The long sentence in a women's prison.

Kat would never survive. Then she thought about the papers – she'd be all over them, front page. She'd be on the news. Paul would be humiliated; he would never speak to her again, never mind see her. Even worse, Kat wouldn't be around for the birth of her first grandchild. She would never get to see her first grandchild. Kat was crying uncontrollably now. Big teardrops spilled from her eyes.

All of this because of a horrible, spiteful, vile little girl. A girl who had caused Kat nothing but pain and misery for no reason whatsoever. A girl who had killed her loving cat—

The blare of a horn jolted Kat back to the present. She had nearly crashed the car. She was halfway home and hadn't remembered one part of the journey. She had nearly veered into oncoming traffic. That would be the end of it all if she had crashed – there was no way she could explain away a dead body lying in the back.

'Honestly, Officer, I thought she was sleeping' wouldn't exactly cut it.

As the evening traffic slowed to a crawl, Kat sneaked a look in her mirror into the back seat. The blanket covered her multitude of sins for now, but she knew she was going to have to deal with this and it had to be sooner rather than later. She had no plan; she was just heading home as she normally did. What the hell was she going to do with the young girl's body lying in the back seat?

Kat wondered if Rachel had any loved ones. Of course she would. Surely she must have a mother and father still alive – she was only late teens or early twenties, after all. She was pretty sure Rachel had a fiancé as well. She vaguely remembered overhearing conversations about him and how great their life together was going to be. How he was going to get her everything she ever wanted. All of this meant one thing: she would be missed. People would be looking for her. She was popular. Her disappearance would most definitely be noticed. Of course it would be. Someone might even phone the police and report her as a missing person. There was no time to waste – Kat had to act fast.

There was no going back now; it had gone way too far. Kat needed to get her act together. She needed to think. To focus. She needed to be smart. She thought of Paul, of the happy news he had brought her; she thought about the joy a grandchild would bring.

Kat had decided. Her mind was made up.

She needed to get away with murder.

20

Kat had two more problems to contend with before she even began to deal with the lifeless girl in the back seat of her car.

The Mercedes had parked in her space yet again, which meant Kat would have to leave her car further down the street. This was far from ideal as she couldn't see the Mini from her window. If something happened to it in the few hours before nightfall then she wouldn't be able to do anything about it. There was no alternative though, so Kat parked the car and tried to avoid her next problem: Mrs Paterson. The wee woman saw everything. She was top of the class when it came to snooping – a veteran curtain twitcher. She was even worse at the moment if that was possible. She had gone into overdrive since she had discovered poor Kiddles and was paying extra attention to Kat. It wasn't as if Kat could just throw Rachel over her shoulder and walk casually into the flat. She was going to have to take her elsewhere. Dispose of her elsewhere, Kat thought with a slight shudder. But for now, Rachel would have to remain covered under the blanket in the back seat. It was risky but then again, what wasn't risky about this whole messed-up situation?

If someone broke into the car tonight they were in for a rude awakening. Kat made sure every last inch of Rachel was still covered by the blanket. She tucked the bottle of bleach and the scrubbing brush under her for good measure. She then had a rethink and rolled Rachel into the footwell with a thud, still completely covered by the blanket. She would be less noticeable down there, especially when it was dark. Or at least Kat hoped that would be the case.

Blood had soaked into the grey back seat and Kat stared at it for a moment. There was a lot of blood. Kat was responsible for this. She had caused it, and now she was going to have to try to clean up her mess. She was going to try to get away with it.

She snapped out of her daze and stood looking through the back window. From outside you couldn't notice the blood or the body. Kat gathered up her things and made her way into the flat. She had two bags now. Her own and Rachel's.

Kat negotiated her way into the flat without bumping into Mrs Paterson, which was a blessing. She was sure that her old neighbour would be watching though. She could feel eyes upon her. Kat opened the door. The flat was completely empty. Completely silent. How she missed Kiddles. Rachel had killed her cat and now inadvertently Kat had killed Rachel. There was some weird circularity about that.

Kat pulled the door closed and then stared in horror at the handle. There was blood on it. Kat looked at her hand. There was blood on that too. Rachel's blood. It brought it all sharply into focus for Kat. This was real.

She made her way to the kitchen sink. She had to get rid of the blood. She needed to get clean. Kat scrubbed her hands vigorously, the water turning a shade of red as it was swept away.

Kat usually headed to the fridge for wine whenever she entered the flat, but tonight more than any other night she needed a clear head. She sat down at the dining-room table and gathered herself together. After a few moments of complete silence, she got up, boiled the kettle and made strong coffee. It was going to be a long night. She needed her wits about her. She needed to cobble together some sort of cohesive plan to deal with this.

Coffee in hand, Kat's attention shifted to Rachel's fancy designer bag. At least she thought it was designer. It looked a hell of a lot fancier and much more expensive than her own. She emptied the contents onto the dining table. A mobile phone, a set of keys, all sorts of make-up, some coins and a pocket knife spilled out.

What the hell was she going to do with a pocket knife?

Kat was now thinking how lucky she had been that Rachel had used her fists to attack her and not the knife. If things had worked out differently, it could have been her lying dead on the car-park floor in a pool of her own blood.

Rachel really was a horrible, vile little girl. What right-minded person takes a knife with them to their work? Especially when you worked in a bank?

Kat slipped everything back into the bag apart from the phone. You could garner a mountain of information about someone by looking into their phone, and she was sure Rachel would be one of those folk whose whole life was on their mobile. She never seemed to be off the thing.

Low and behold, the iPhone was locked though. It was one of those blasted things with the thumb pad for your fingerprint. By hook or by crook she was going to get into it. A wicked thought flashed into Kat's head. She had Rachel's fingerprints – she had Rachel's fingers, for goodness' sake. Kat turned the device off for now.

Kat suddenly paused – she should be wearing gloves at the very least when she was dissecting a dead girl's handbag. She hadn't even considered it. She tipped the contents back out and grabbed a pair of washing-up gloves. She sprayed all the items and the bag with a disinfectant spray and wiped them all down as best she could. It was far from ideal, but it would have to do.

Kat really needed to come up with a plan; she needed to think clearly about what she was going to do next. It wasn't as if she could follow some clear protocol. Obviously, she hadn't dealt with anything remotely like this before, but she needed to be smarter. She needed to be more careful. At this rate, the evidence was stacking up against her and there was no chance of getting away with it.

She would have to wait until it was darker outside to deal with Rachel. Mrs Paterson was bound to be keeping watch at this hour. She would be ready to pounce. Kat had been lucky to avoid her on the way in, but she would definitely be on the lookout by now. Her old neighbour would combust if she knew what was really going on next door.

Maybe a little glass of wine was a good idea, after all – Kat's nerves definitely needed settled. Or maybe Kat was making excuses so she could have a drink. She had started depending on the bottle far too much lately.

It was then that a horrible thought hit her like a ton of bricks.

The CCTV.

Oh God, the CCTV in the car park.

It would have captured everything.

21

I can't believe she agreed to do it. I thought men were easy to manipulate, but for fuck's sake, Rachel never even put up a fight. No wonder she's got a reputation for being such a slut. I bet you don't even have to buy her dinner.

Hats off to her though – she played a blinder. Those drama classes when she was younger certainly paid off. The way she tells it, Fat Kat fell for it hook, line and sinker. She thought everything was going to be hunky-dory. How daft can you be?

The fat cow was off for a few days due to her 'grief'. It was a poxy cat. It's not like it was her son or her old mum. I didn't know it would work as well as it did on the little fucker. Thought it might get sick or something, but it worked way too good. It was a pleasant little bonus. Wonder if it works on humans?

Kat must be realising now that it's not going to stop. That it's going to get worse. With any luck, she'll drink herself to death. Rachel told me the whole flat was a mess and reeked of booze so I'd say we're definitely getting to her. On second thoughts, if she done herself in then the plan would be ruined and the fun would be over. Who knows who might get their paws on what's owed to us?

There's plenty more planned. The fat bitch had a good run working in the bank, but it's coming to an end. She's going to realise soon enough that this can't go on.

I'll not stop until she's paid for all that she's done.

22

There was no way Kat could check the underground car park CCTV at this time of night. It would certainly raise suspicion if she arrived at work out of hours. She would have to wait until the morning. Hopefully, all she was about to do tonight wouldn't be in vain. It couldn't wait though. It needed to be done.

It was around midnight before Kat had gathered up the courage to put her hastily convened plan into action. She had been having major doubts about the whole thing and had seriously considered handing herself in to the local police office. Tell them exactly what had happened and confess to her moment of madness afterwards. However, as it turned out, she didn't have the courage for that either.

The thought of Paul and her forthcoming grandchild was always at the forefront of her mind. The thought of what the little witch had done to poor Kiddles was etched there as well. She hoped he hadn't suffered.

This needed to be done. It was too late to go back now.

Kat, dressed all in black, walked cautiously to her car. She had felt ridiculous dressing herself like a cat burglar from an old black-and-white film but she had thought it only practical for what lay ahead.

She walked steadily past the Mercedes, still infuriatingly in her spot, to the end of the road and opened the car door. She slid into the driver's seat. Mrs Paterson's curtains didn't even twitch. Surely her nosy neighbour would be sleeping at this hour? There was no one in the street; it was eerily silent.

In the few hours that had passed since Rachel's death, Kat had tried to go over all the possibilities and eventualities. She couldn't believe that this was actually happening, but she needed to get her act together. The police had no reason to come looking for her or to link her in any way to Rachel. Not yet anyway. However, if they did somehow put it together, Kat had to close any loose ends that might lead to her guilt being exposed. There was no reason for anyone to suspect that Kat was capable of murder, but she had to be careful. One small oversight on her part could lead to her being arrested. She had to pray the CCTV wouldn't be her undoing.

She had spent a considerable amount of time listing as many secluded places as she could think of to dispose of Rachel's body, but she kept coming back to the same venue. For all intents and purposes, it was an ideal location.

Years ago, Kat had camped out in woods on the outskirts of Glasgow with her then husband and they had joked with each other that they could do anything they wanted there as no one would ever happen upon them. They could even dump a body there and no one would find it, Stephen had said, laughing. Little did she know back then, the next time she came back, she actually *would* be disposing of a body. You couldn't make it up.

Kat and Stephen had come to the woods as they were after privacy, and Stephen couldn't afford to book a hotel never mind a holiday. However, it had been a great weekend, back when Stephen wasn't a complete arse. Back then, they'd had no money whatsoever, but staying in a tent, just the two of them, had been perfect, even though the place they pitched their tent was a complete and utter dump. Stephen had reasoned that it was cheap and cheerful and was only a fifteen-minute drive so wouldn't cost much in the way of petrol. This also suited Kat's much darker purpose tonight.

She had decided that this complete and utter dump was the perfect place, where Rachel could remain for some time without being found. As far as Kat could remember, the spot wasn't even popular with dog walkers, so there was every chance the body would lay undiscovered for a considerable period of time. However, just in case she was found sooner, Kat had brought along a few things to remove any evidence that she had ever been involved. Or at least muddy the waters a little. There was sure to be some of Kat's DNA on the body and that wouldn't do. There could be no trace left. Nothing that would make the police suspect Kat or come looking for her.

The drive took Kat around twenty-five minutes as she took two wrong turnings. Her mind was going into overdrive and she had lost concentration. On the way, she was having an internal argument with herself. She knew things had gone too far; she knew this was all wrong, but still she pressed on. This was her last chance to stop. However, no one would understand if she confessed now. There was no valid explanation for any of this. There was no going back.

Kat parked the car on the edge of the wood, turned off the lights and waited. There wasn't a soul in sight and the place looked as if it hadn't been visited in years. It was overgrown and inhospitable. Kat exited the car.

First of all, she had to gain access to Rachel's phone.

Kat slid open the back door and brought out the phone. She turned it on and pressed Rachel's thumb to the keypad. After a tense moment, the handset came to life.

She then went into the settings, removed the fingerprint setting and changed the keypad entry to 0000 so she could look at the phone later and not be hurried. She turned it off again and placed it in the glove compartment of the car and set about the real matter at hand.

Kat spotted a few felled trees not too far into the woods. They would make a decent enough final resting place for her tormentor. There was no way Kat was going to dig any sort of shallow grave, so the trees would help to keep her hidden. It wasn't perfect, but it would have to do.

This was it. Now or never. Kat humphed Rachel over her shoulder and walked with her to the trees. Thank the lord Rachel was a slight thing.

She dumped the body between the two fallen trees and stood back. Unless you were standing directly over the body, there was no way you could tell she was there.

Now was the part Kat had been dreading. The part she had been going over and over in her head. The part of the plan she had reasoned needed to be done. She moved back to the car and returned with bottles of bleach, white spirit and a full petrol can. She was determined no trace of her would be left behind for the police to find.

Kat took a deep breath then started pouring bleach all over the body. Three full bottles went over her – she even rolled the body and poured bleach on her back and the ground where she lay. The white spirit went on next. She gave special attention to Rachel's fingers; there would surely be traces of Kat on them after they had grappled in the car park. Rachel's bag and possessions were drenched as well.

The petrol went on last.

How had it come to this?

Tears were streaming freely from Kat's eyes. Rachel's body was swimming in bleach, white spirit and petrol.

Kat lifted a small dirty rag and set it on fire with the cheap lighter she had brought along.

They were deep enough into the woods that the fire wouldn't draw any attention. At least, Kat hoped that was the case. This was it. Kat closed her eyes and threw the rag onto Rachel. Right away, the fire took a fierce hold. There was definitely no turning back now.

Kat stood back and watched. The last thing she wanted was for the fire to spread and burn down the whole forest, but thankfully it stayed confined to the spot where she had placed Rachel.

Horrible thoughts flooded into Kat's head. Rachel could remain here for months before someone stumbled upon her, and by then there might not be much left. There was bound to be plenty of wildlife in these woods, plus the fire and bleach would have made her unrecognisable. These dark thoughts surprised her.

Never in a million years did Kat think she'd be spending her night doing this. Never in a million years did Kat think she'd be capable of such dark deeds. She tried to keep telling herself that it had been an accident and this was necessary to avoid her life being ruined as well. Rachel had brought this on herself, after all. If she hadn't confronted and attacked Kat in the car park then none of this would have happened. The horrible sequence of events wouldn't have been set in motion. Kat wouldn't be standing in the middle of nowhere watching fire engulf a young girl's body.

Everything had spiralled completely out of control.

23

Kat sat in her car at the edge of the woods. The blood-soaked back seat and footwell were now empty.

Kat knew she should be getting out of there quick smart but she couldn't move. She was crying uncontrollably. Tears streamed down her face. She felt as if she was going to pass out or be sick. She was thinking about Rachel, thinking about the bleach, the petrol and the fire engulfing her body. Her face. How had it come to this? More so though, Kat was thinking about her poor cat, about Paul and Charlotte's good news. What a terrible, terrible mess. For a moment, she felt as if another panic attack was on the way. She concentrated on her breathing, as she had been taught at the hospital. The feelings eventually passed and slowly she regained her composure. There was no going back now, and this certainly wasn't the time to sit mulling things over.

Get a grip, Kat told herself. She took another deep breath and gathered herself together before finally driving away and on to the next stage of her plan. Time was of the essence.

Kat knew she had to get rid of the car. There was no getting away from it. The amount of forensic evidence would be frightening and very damning. If she kept it then further down the line, if she was ever thought of as a suspect in the murder, it would be searched. Then it would be over and all of this would have been for nothing. It would be foolish in the extreme to even think about keeping it.

Kat had what some would consider a stockpile of cleaning products in the flat due to her mild OCD and she was going to put them to good use. She was determined no trace of Rachel would be left behind and the police would have no reason to come calling at her door or link her to the crime.

She drove the car to a patch of wasteland in Maryhill which she had identified when planning earlier in the night. She was sure the large area was no stranger to burnt-out cars. It was close enough to the flat for her to walk home and out of the way enough to mean it wouldn't be found immediately.

By the time she set to work on the car, it was the small hours of the morning and Kat was well aware that she still had to go to work and act as if nothing was unusual or out of the ordinary.

The barren patch of waste ground lay quiet and still. Kat got to work. Hopefully her luck would hold and no one would come near.

She scrubbed the car ferociously. The bleach and cleaning products covered every inch of the Mini. Kat's eyes were stinging and she was finding it hard to breathe. She should have brought one of the little white masks she'd used for painting her bedroom. Kat had focused her efforts mostly on the back seat where Rachel had lain for so long. She scrubbed the back seats and footwells with vigour, but the bloodstains were a nightmare to shift. The forthcoming fire would have to take care of that. Hopefully, no one would be searching for any sign of Rachel in the car anyway – they had no reason to do so, but if they did Kat had done her level best to eliminate any trace.

Kat poured liberal amounts of bleach over the clothes she was wearing when the deadly deed was committed and the black clothes she was wearing to dispose of the body. She had brought a change of clothing in a black bag that she hoped would not be contaminated by any evidence. She took Rachel's phone from the glove compartment and placed it beside her clean clothes.

The petrol went on the car next. Kat was getting worryingly good at covering her tracks considering this was so out of character for her. She dropped her gloves into the petrol-and-bleach-covered car for good measure. She threw in the rag this time and jumped back as the fire rapidly engulfed the car and nearly scorched her eyebrows clean off. It was well and truly ablaze. She hoped there wouldn't be a huge explosion that might be heard and seen for miles.

The wasteland was far enough away that the car hopefully wouldn't be found for a while and the evidence would be obliterated. Well, that was the plan anyway. It wasn't like Kat had done this before. She was winging it.

Kat changed into her new set of clothes, put the hood of her jacket up and headed for the flat as quick as she could, praying she wouldn't bump into anyone. It was unlikely given the early hour, but you never knew who was watching.

She was sweating profusely even though it was cold at this hour. She walked as fast as her overweight body allowed and tried not to think of what had just happened. What she had just done. She turned things over in her mind. It wasn't even murder, she thought – if anything it was self-defence, culpable homicide they would call it maybe. Although, now she had gone that crucial step further and got rid of the body in a cold, calculated manner. There was no way she could put that down to any sort of accident. It had been planned and carried out with alarming swiftness and efficiency. Pre-meditated the police would say. Had she always been capable of such deeds or had Rachel pushed her so far that she had snapped? This clearly wasn't normal behaviour.

Kat couldn't get Rachel's face out of her mind. The image of herself pouring bleach onto the body and the flames flashed into her head and wouldn't shift. It was imprinted on her brain. The smell of burning flesh and bleach would remain with her until she met her maker, she was sure of that.

The weird thing was though, Kat wasn't sure who she was feeling sorrier for – Rachel or herself?

24

As Kat walked home the heavens opened. The rain lashed down on her and there were rumbles of thunder. It seemed appropriate. It summed up the whole dark mood of the evening perfectly.

Kat hoped the rain wouldn't put out the fires before all the evidence had been completely destroyed, then she scolded herself internally – who the hell was she anymore? How could Kat be capable of these thoughts? How could she be capable of these dark deeds? How had this been allowed to happen? Things had spiralled completely out of control.

It took Kat around half an hour to walk back to the flat, and she was absolutely drenched and exhausted by the time she put her key in the door. Her luck was holding for once – no one was around because of the rain and the early hour. She stripped off her sodden clothes and threw them in the washing machine in case any fibres had transferred their way onto her.

Whilst the washing machine spun, Kat went for a hot shower. She stood under the shower head for much longer than usual. She felt numb as she went over everything that had happened over the past few days. No amount of hot water could wash away her sins.

She knew she wouldn't be able to sleep. There wasn't much point in trying anyway, as she was due to leave for work in a couple of hours. Her mind was doing overtime in any case. Kat couldn't help thinking she had forgotten something that would incriminate her and bring the whole thing tumbling down.

The car park CCTV was the main problem now, and she was going to grab the bull by the horns and deal with that first thing this morning. If the CCTV had been positioned to take in Kat's car then it was over – all of this had been for nothing and Kat would duly be arrested for murder and for trying to cover up said murder in an extreme way that no one would comprehend. There would be no explaining it away. Kat's life as she knew it would be over. All she could do was hope and pray that the cameras had been facing another area of the car park.

She would find out soon enough.

Kat sat on her couch in the complete silence and darkness of her flat. How she missed Kiddles. She eventually rose and began to get ready to face the world again as if nothing out of the ordinary had happened. If the CCTV was going to bring her down, she was better finding out sooner rather than later. There was no point putting it off.

Kat had a phone call to make before she left for work and dealt with the CCTV though.

'Which service do you require?'

'Police, please. I'd like to report a stolen car…'

25

It's no wonder hardly anyone seemed to report crime these days. The rigmarole on the phone dealing with the police operator was very stressful indeed. Kat would have given up if she hadn't been trying so hard to cover her tracks. She only wanted to report her car as stolen but it took forever.

The woman on the phone was nice enough, but she asked some frankly ridiculous questions. She had even asked if there was any chance Kat had just misplaced her car. She had nearly said, 'Hold on a minute and I'll just see if it's fallen down the side of the couch,' but she had restrained herself. Kat didn't want to be remembered so tried not to say anything out of the ordinary or memorable.

Her car was obviously not a top priority. They said someone would be out within the next day or two and she was told not to hold out much hope for the vehicle's safe return. Kat felt as if she was wasting police time. They just seemed happy to give her a crime report number and be done with it. The phone call didn't exactly inspire confidence in Police Scotland. All of which suited Kat just fine. She didn't want the car found promptly – she hoped the car would never be found.

*

Kat's journey to work took a little longer this morning due to not having her car. She took the subway from Kelvinbridge to Buchanan Street and then walked the short distance to the bank. It was a journey filled with trepidation as to what awaited her. This could be the last time she enjoyed the fresh air and freedom for a long while if things went badly. It may have been a crisp, cold morning but Kat didn't feel the chill. So much rested on what was going to happen this morning.

Kat arrived at work. She walked round to the side of the bank, where the entrance to the underground car park was.

This was it. The moment her actions came crashing down. Or the moment getting away with murder became real.

She headed straight to the little security booth, where an older man sat reading a dog-eared paperback. He looked on the verge of sleep. Kat knew the security man had worked there for years but he was either very shy or very ignorant because he barely said two words to anyone. Kat had, to her knowledge, never had a conversation with him in all the time she had worked there. He always looked bored to tears, and who could blame him? Watching over an underground car park for a living wasn't likely to be the most exciting or challenging job in the world.

Kat took a deep breath then knocked on the door and entered.

'Hi, I was wondering if you could help me out?' Kat said, hoping her nerves wouldn't come across. This could be a pivotal moment in her life. It could change the entire course of it forever.

'What's the problem, darling?' the security guard asked. He didn't look like he would be able to offer much security to anyone. He was barely fighting sleep.

'It's nothing really. It's just… there was a small scratch on my car last night and I was just wondering if the CCTV showed anyone hitting it?'

The security guard looked forlorn; he wasn't used to actually doing anything in this role. He must have been at a good part in his novel, as he didn't want to part with it. Kat wondered if he actually knew how to go back and check the tapes or if it was all linked to a computer. Either way, the guy looked as if he'd rather be having dental surgery than help Kat.

'Do you know what time last night?' he said. 'That would help me narrow it down.'

'I do as it happens; it was between 6 p.m. and 6.30 p.m.'

The security guard looked surprised – he wasn't expecting a time, especially such a narrow time frame. He even put down his book, although he didn't look very happy at having to do so.

'I'd been down to my car for some papers at 6 p.m. and the car was fine, then I left the building at 6.30 p.m. and there was a scratch on it,' Kat offered as further explanation. Not that it was really needed – the security guy was barely listening.

'Okay, I'll have a look at the system. Where was the motor parked?'

'It was parked in bay three.' Kat hoped he wasn't noting all of this down.

The man fiddled with the screens in front of him and after a few minutes of agonising searching and muttered cursing, he had found the desired time frame. Kat tried to breathe normally.

'Right, here we are.'

Kat braced herself for what was said next. This was it. She held her breath. Everything rested on this.

'No… nope, you're out of luck, sweetheart. The camera was pointing elsewhere between 6 p.m. and 7 p.m. I'm really sorry, love,' he said, smiling. He was one step closer to getting rid of Kat and returning to his novel.

'No, no, it's fine – it was just out of curiosity. Don't worry about it,' Kat said, edging out of the door. She could have hugged him.

Kat hoped her sense of relief wasn't showing on her face. She needn't have worried though – the security guard ushered her out and went back to his book. Kat was already forgotten about.

Kat left the little booth and stopped to think for a moment. She smiled. For the first time since this whole sorry episode began, Kat thought she might just get away with it.

26

Kat slowly made her way up the stairs from the underground car park to work. She had had enough of the lift to last her a lifetime, plus she was in no rush to get into the office. However, it wasn't through fears of bullying. Kat was weighing up all that had taken place. So much had happened in such a short period of time and she knew that nothing would ever be the same again.

It was strange. She had been going through a whole range of emotions since the fateful incident, and she couldn't rid Rachel's burning image from her mind. Kat knew she was responsible for a young girl's life prematurely coming to an end, but if she was being honest with herself, she felt as if a weight had been lifted from her shoulders. It was relief. Relief that she would no longer have to put up with Rachel and the bullying in work, or anywhere else for that matter. Relief that the CCTV hadn't recorded what had happened and she wouldn't be spending the rest of her days in prison. Relief that seeing her grandchildren being born hadn't been snatched away from her. Kat knew this feeling wasn't normal. Surely she should be a quivering wreck after what had happened?

Kat made herself a coffee and sat at her desk. An hour or so into her shift she heard a few of her colleagues talking about Rachel and for a horrible moment thought she had been found already. That would scupper her plan in its infancy. However, they were only wondering where she was. Obviously, she hadn't turned up for work this morning. Only Kat knew the reason why. Only Kat knew that she would never be turning up for work ever again.

Kat sneaked away to the toilets but not for a cry as she usually did. She was going to text Tony, the inept manager, and buy herself some time. The text wouldn't be from her own phone though; it would be from Rachel's. She really should have done this earlier, but the CCTV had taken up the majority of her time and thoughts. Now that was taken care of, Kat could concentrate on other matters.

It was extremely risky carrying Rachel's phone around with her, but Kat needed to get a good look at it and she hadn't had a chance as yet. She knew she should get rid of the thing, but in the back of her mind she had a thought that if she could convince a few people Rachel was still alive and well then it would work out better for her. Or it would prolong the agony. Either way, she was going to inspect it.

Kat scrolled through Rachel's contacts until she came to Tony M. She thumbed her way into texts so she could compose a new message to him. There were loads of messages between the pair of them already on the phone. Kat couldn't believe what she was reading.

Rachel and Tony were having an affair. There was absolutely no doubt about it – the messages were filthy.

Oh my God – there were photos!

Kat composed a message quickly. She had been in the toilet for longer than she realised – time flew by when you were reading someone's explicit messages. She sent the small text to Tony – trying her best to copy Rachel's phrasing and style.

Not coming in today. Can you cover for me? See you soon –
look forward to next meet lol xx

Kat put the phone back in her bag, making doubly sure it was switched off. She couldn't wait to further inspect it at lunch and after work. What else would she uncover if she had stumbled upon an affair between Rachel and her manager within two minutes of turning the thing on?

Back at her desk, Kat couldn't help smiling. Today was going to be a good day – she was absolutely sure about that. She smiled at the knowledge of Rachel and Tony's affair. She smiled at the thought that Rachel would never bother her again.

27

Kat couldn't concentrate at all in the office. All she could focus on was Rachel's phone. She needed to see what else was on it and she needed to do it today. She absolutely had to get rid of it as soon as possible.

At lunchtime, Kat tried to find somewhere quiet where she could look at the phone in peace. However, her options were limited. She couldn't sit in her car anymore as she'd got rid of it, and she didn't want to sit in the toilet for her lunch hour. The canteen was too busy and she couldn't take the chance that someone would see something they shouldn't or notice that she had a different phone today. Or worse still, notice that she had Rachel's phone.

Kat walked out from the bank onto Bothwell Street and found a little cafe which didn't look too busy. It didn't look too welcoming either. The paint peeled from the walls and the place looked in dire need of a makeover. There were a couple of high chairs at the window which allowed patrons to sit with their food. The lack of customers suited Kat just fine though. All she wanted was a bit of privacy.

She paid for a dubious-looking salad roll and a coffee which looked like black sludge and took a seat. Time was moving on. Kat pulled out Rachel's phone and read whilst nibbling at her roll. From the moment she turned the device on, she was being constantly interrupted with phone calls and notifications from people eager to get in contact with Rachel. This emphasised the need to ditch the phone. It was only a matter of time before she was reported missing.

Kat was reading messages between Rachel and her fiancé Jason whilst trying to digest her roll. The coffee tasted as bad as it looked. It was clear from the messages that there wasn't much love around for a couple who were meant to be tying the knot soon. They were constantly arguing and sniping at each other, and the last two messages indicated that something significant had happened very recently. Kat took it that Jason had hit Rachel after he had been provoked somehow.

Rachel: 'You do that to me again and you'll be sorry.'
Jason: 'I didn't mean it but don't fuckin threatn me.'

Kat was thinking how she could use this information to her advantage somehow, but the idea would have to wait. Time flew by when you were perusing a dead girl's phone and Kat realised she had to get back to the office. Her lunch break was just about over.

Throughout the afternoon, Kat kept nipping off to the toilet for brief looks at the phone. No one seemed to notice. However, every time Kat turned the handset on someone invariably phoned, which meant she had to wait for the call to end and couldn't look at the messages. It was incredibly frustrating. She knew time was limited, as the longer she kept Rachel's phone, the higher the chance of her being caught with it in her possession.

*

Kat's work day was almost at an end. It hadn't been as productive as she'd hoped. She had been thinking about all the events over the past few days, but she hadn't managed to look at the phone as much as she would've liked. She couldn't concentrate on work, and if management looked into what she had achieved today then she was for the high jump. Fortunately, it was only Tony who could check up on her, and he was far too lazy to get involved.

Kat looked again at the email advertising for the team manager's job to replace naughty Tony. Kat knew she could do the job far better than he could. What was stopping her? How could she even be thinking about her career prospects at a time like this? She had just disposed of her young colleague's body hours before, yet here she was looking into the possibility of gaining a promotion at work. Her mind was muddled. She'd been through a hell of a lot over the past few days. Applying for a promotion at work wasn't a big deal in the grand scheme of things. What's the worst that could happen? No time like the present.

Kat followed the link to the job advert and clicked 'Apply'.

28

Looks like Rachel's bottle has well and truly crashed. She never made it to work today. I talked to Tony about it and he said she'd text him but she never bothered to text me. He's been a bit funny as well. Went a bit weird when I questioned him about Rachel. Why's she texting him and not me anyway? They're not even that friendly. If it wasn't for me then Tony wouldn't have given her the job.

She'll be back in a few days I reckon, once she's realised what a drama queen she's being. Once she's calmed down. She shouldn't have agreed to do it if she wasn't up for it. It's not like I forced her – well, not this time.

She needs to get her shit together. For God's sake, it was only a cat.

She knows why we're doing this. She knows the end game. Not that she's going to benefit much out of it. But fuck it, I can't be worrying about that.

29

Kat knew that mobile phones could be tracked. For this reason, she had decided that she wasn't going to risk turning the phone on in her flat and alerting the police to her location. At the very least it could let them know that the phone had been in her flat for a prolonged period of time when they inevitably started to investigate Rachel's disappearance or murder.

After work, she decided to head back to the dingy coffee shop, which was open to 6 p.m. even though customers seemed to be scarce. That gave her just under an hour to get as much information from the mobile as possible before she got rid of the thing once and for all. She bought another dubious-looking coffee and settled down at her window seat with some much needed privacy.

Kat sipped at the sludge they passed off as coffee. She had plugged Rachel's phone into the charger she had picked up from the newsagents next door; she didn't want to be in the middle of reading some juicy messages when the blasted battery died. She then took out a pen and notepad in case she felt the need to jot anything down and got to work. Already she had uncovered an affair between Rachel and her boss and a possible instance of domestic abuse at the hands of Jason. What else awaited her?

Kat needed to work fast as the cafe was closing soon and she really had to get rid of the phone. If she was found with it in her possession, everything would have been for nothing and the whole sorry mess would come crashing down. She just hoped that no one would be actively looking for, or tracking, the phone yet.

The messages from Tony were damning. There was no way it wasn't exactly what it looked like. They had been at it for a good while. The first message on the phone from him was from months ago and you could see them escalating. Tony had arranged the job for Rachel in the first place. She wondered if there was even the need for a job interview. Then she shuddered at how an interview between the pair of them might have played out.

Some of the photos were truly disgusting, but Kat couldn't help but look. Tony was obviously very proud of certain parts of his anatomy. She had seen more than enough of him. She wondered how she would look him in the eye from now on or how she would manage to keep a straight face when she saw him next in work. Then Kat wondered how she could use this new-found information to her advantage. Kat had never had such devious thoughts before in her life.

The next person in the message list was someone called Ste.

Kat thumbed her way into the messages. Oh my God, Rachel was seeing this Ste guy as well. The texts made it clear. It wasn't just the pair of them being flirty – they were talking about things that had actually happened between them and looking forward to further encounters.

So she was seeing Tony, Ste and she had Jason, her fiancé. What a little slut she was. Who else was she with?

There were no photos in this message thread, which surprisingly disappointed Kat. She was actually beginning to enjoy herself. The messages and photos had her transfixed.

Kat read further…

Then spilled her coffee everywhere.

30

Kat stared at the phone. Somehow her mug hadn't smashed but coffee now covered the grimy floor. Thankfully, the cafe owner seemed to be too busy cleaning up through the back, judging by the noisy clanging of pots and pans, to take any notice of his only customer and the mess she had made. Kat looked in disbelief at the message sent by Ste.

> We don't want your mother finding out. You're my
> stepdaughter, after all – it would be frowned upon! x

Ste was Rachel's stepfather! What the hell had she stumbled upon? Rachel and her stepdad? Kat scrolled further and read on with horror.

There was no doubt about it. Rachel was having an affair with her stepdad. What age was Ste? What did it matter? It was wrong on so many different levels. Kat was engrossed in the phone – this was better than any soap opera her mother loved watching. This was real life in all its messed-up, sordid glory.

Kat couldn't take her eyes from the messages. The two of them didn't care one bit about Rachel's mother/Ste's wife. They were actually laughing at her, saying she had no clue what was happening and that she was too daft to ever catch them. They were making fun of her. Maybe Mrs Strang should be told exactly what had been going on right under her nose? Maybe she should be told, in detail, what her no-good scumbag of a husband and her lovely daughter had been up to.

The phone buzzed in her hand. Kat nearly jumped out of her skin. Jason, the fiancé, was phoning. She let the phone ring out. There was no way she could possibly answer it, after all. She set the phone aside until the buzzing ended and grabbed some napkins to try to clean up the coffee on the floor. When she returned her attention to the mobile, a small icon had appeared indicating that Jason had left a voice message. Kat thumbed her way through and listened to it.

'What's going on, Rach? Why you not answering or phoning me back? Getting worried here. At least send me a text, let me know you're alright. I know I shouldn't have hit you but… just phone me back, eh?'

The voicemail confirmed Kat's suspicions that Jason had hit Rachel. So much for their supposed idyllic life together. What a nasty little temper Jason had. Maybe he should be told what his fiancée was up to? His beloved wife-to-be was having two affairs, one of which was with her bloody stepfather. How would he react to that bombshell?

Kat stopped and stared at the phone. Maybe everyone involved in this mess should be told exactly what was going on. An idea was forming in her head and she allowed herself a little smile. Was she really that devious?

Every few minutes or so, Rachel's phone either received a message or a phone call. It was eating into Kat's time looking at the thing. Kat was lucky if her own phone went once a day, and it was normally a nuisance call trying to talk about the accident she had never been involved in. She rarely received any messages from her friends anymore. The volume of calls and texts on Rachel's phone reinforced to Kat that she absolutely had to get rid of it and quickly. No excuses. It was only a matter of time before she was reported missing and the phone might be tracked.

She decided to try to stop the phone being traced, although she wasn't sure it would work. She put the device into airplane mode which disabled Wi-Fi and the network, and would stop any incoming calls, which were drastically reducing her time reading Rachel's messages. She also disabled the GPS – or at least she hoped that she had. It was still too risky to turn the phone on at home though, she thought. If she looked at the phone in work or in Glasgow city centre then it wouldn't be anything out of the ordinary and it wouldn't flag up that Rachel's phone had been in Kat's flat for an extended period of time. Kat thought it must really have been a hell of a lot easier to get away with crimes in years gone by without smartphones tracking your every step, CCTV watching your every move and forensic scientists examining every tiny fibre and hair and God knows what else on your body.

31

Kat couldn't get in the door quick enough. She needed peace and quiet to dissect what she had read on Rachel's phone and time was of the essence. Kat had no car so she was later home than usual, which was annoying but couldn't be helped. She still noticed that the rude young guy with the expensive suit and even more expensive Mercedes had stolen her space yet again. But Kat couldn't worry about that just now – she had higher priorities. Much higher priorities.

Kat really didn't need to see Mrs Paterson tonight, but there she was hanging around as usual, eagerly awaiting her arrival home from work.

'Kat, where's that car of yours?' she asked as soon as Kat was within earshot.

'Hi, Mrs Paterson. It's getting fixed at the garage again. No luck with it at the moment!' Kat wanted rid of Mrs Paterson as quickly as possible; she didn't want to answer any more questions, and telling her the car had been stolen would have elicited further interrogation. Telling her what had really happened to the car would have resulted in an ambulance being called.

'How are you feeling? You want to come in for your tea? I've made beef stew with dumplings.' Mrs Paterson had taken to cooking for Kat since Kiddles had died.

'I'm fine. Thanks for the offer but I'm okay tonight – maybe another time though.' Kat backed away from her neighbour and into the flat.

'I'll hold you to that!' Mrs Paterson shouted.

Kat stepped inside the sanctuary of her flat and closed the door. Made doubly sure it was locked.

Mrs Paterson meant well, but she was an irritation Kat could well do without at the moment. Things were stressful enough without having to deal with nosy neighbours. Even if they were cooking her dinner.

*

Kat turned over in her head what she had seen on Rachel's phone. An affair with her manager at the bank was bad enough, but now she had uncovered an affair between Rachel and her stepfather. Plus, she had found out more about Rachel and Jason's volatile and sometimes violent relationship. She had spent the whole night trying to digest the sordid contents and it was now the small hours. Kat had also resolved to get rid of the phone tomorrow, although as yet she hadn't come up with a reasonable plan to dispose of it.

She had to stop and get at least some sleep. She hadn't even stopped for dinner.

One good thing might come out of all this heartache and stress however – she might lose a bit of weight. Kat laughed then made her way to bed, though she knew sleep would be hard to come by. She had to try though; her alarm would sound in less than four hours.

32

Kat woke with a start. She must have dozed off after all. She had hardly slept a wink since the fateful incident. The unexpected vibration of her phone as it buzzed on her bedside table drew Kat sharply from sleep. For a horrible moment, she thought it might have been Rachel's phone buzzing, but then she remembered she had made doubly sure it was turned off. Kat's phone hardly ever received calls or texts, especially now that Rachel wouldn't be sending her any more abusive messages.

Kat sat up and looked at the message which had come through. It was from the dating site Rachel had signed her up to confirming that her account was now closed and giving her a link to reactivate her profile if she should so wish. Not bloody likely.

Kat jumped in for a shower and got ready quickly. She was going to leave for work early. This was one of her last opportunities to have a look at Rachel's phone before she got rid of it once and for all tonight. It was frustrating not being able to peruse it at her leisure at home, but there was no way she was going to risk alerting the police to her involvement.

She entered the cafe, of which she was now becoming a regular customer. The same guy had served her every time she had been in, but he looked completely disinterested and didn't want to strike up a conversation. Kat decided against a coffee and opted for a small carton of orange juice. She sat down at her favourite spot and took out Rachel's phone. Within thirty seconds of turning it on, it was buzzing with messages and missed-call alerts. There were loads of them. Kat realised this couldn't go on much longer. She needed to get rid of the phone. She was bound to slip up if she sent any more messages trying to pretend they were from Rachel. There were fourteen missed-call alerts. Fourteen! Six from Jason, four from her mum, two from Kirsty and two from unknown numbers. Kat knew it was foolish holding on to the phone. It would end up getting her caught.

Kat thumbed her way into the messages. The latest one was from her manager and secret lover Tony.

> What's going on? You coming into work today? How come no text or meet last night? Missed ya xx

Tony really was smitten with her. She composed a reply to Tony and hoped it would buy her some more time. Tony wasn't the sharpest tool in the box so it shouldn't be too hard. She told him she would be back at work tomorrow and to cover for her again, and promised she would make it up to him.

The problem with the phone was that there was just too much information on it and Kat felt she had barely scratched the surface. So far, she had uncovered two affairs, one of which was with Rachel's stepfather, so who knew what else she would find?

She just didn't have the time to look through everything on it and taking a few days off work at this point might raise suspicion further down the line. She promised herself she would deal with the phone tonight; she'd dispose of it.

Kat was just about to switch the phone off and make her way out into the street to walk to work when it buzzed again. It was another text message.

The sender was Kirsty.

> Listen, get back to work TODAY. You killed her cat – it's no big deal. We'll sort it. Okay, I shouldn't have made you do it. Happy now?

Kat stared at the message. She felt the anger rise up within her.

Kirsty had made Rachel do it. Kirsty had made Rachel enter her flat and kill her poor cat.

Kirsty was the orchestrator.

33

I shouldn't have made you do it.

It was Kirsty. All along, it was her.

Kat had thought Rachel was the ringleader. Mistakenly thought Rachel was the ringleader. She seemed to instigate every instance of bullying. Now, Kat had discovered she was being manipulated and ordered around by Kirsty.

Rachel had started the verbal abuse in work, but it was always Kirsty who was the most vocal cheerleader, and on occasion Kirsty had started the abuse herself.

Kat couldn't suppress her anger about this revelation. She was glad Rachel was no longer going to be an issue, but surely she didn't deserve to die? It had been an accident, self-defence even, but it would have taken a hell of a lot of explaining away. Rachel had tormented her for months and she had entered her home and killed her cat. There was no getting away from that. Yet, did she deserve her fate? Did she deserve to be left in woods covered in bleach, white spirit and petrol and then set alight? Did anyone deserve such a fate? Was she forced to do all of this by Kirsty? How much hold over someone could you have that they could force you to do such a horrible thing?

Kat stared at the message on the handset. Her grip hardened on the phone as her anger rose. She wished Kirsty had ended up the same way as Rachel, if she was being honest. Kat surprised herself with this thinking – she had never thought like this before. The bullying and death of her cat seemed to have triggered these dark thoughts.

Kirsty had to be dealt with. She couldn't be allowed to get away scot-free for destroying Kat's life. Kat wasn't going to kill her. The first time had been a fluke; the second time would be a disaster and premeditated. Anyway, who was Kat kidding? She was no killer.

Kirsty wouldn't be as strong without her little minion Rachel to protect her and back her up, and there was no way Kat was going to allow the bullying to continue after what had happened. She had been through too much for it all to be for nothing.

Kat looked at the messages on the phone between Kirsty and Rachel. The two of them were working in tandem to ruin Kat's life but why? What reason could they possibly have for choosing her and not someone else in the office? Was Kat just the unlucky one who had been picked out at random or had she done something to upset the pair? The language they used in the messages about her was vile. Why did they hate her so much?

Kat didn't have enough time to continue reading the conversations; she was already going to be late. She needed to get into the office, although she wasn't sure Tony would notice if she was there or not. The message from Kirsty had thrown her completely off course. She had to be smart and stay calm. She needed to cobble together some sort of plan to deal with this.

She needed to stop Kirsty once and for all.

34

One good thing about Tony's complete inability to perform the duties of a manager was that he didn't notice Kat disappearing for prolonged periods of time throughout the day to check Rachel's phone. This was her only chance to look at the phone as she had to dump it tonight before it led to her capture and arrest. She'd already held on to it for far too long.

Kat had been in work for a couple of hours, but her mind had been elsewhere. She couldn't stop thinking about the message from Kirsty and was going over all possible scenarios in her head. One thing was for sure – Kat couldn't allow the bullying to continue. Not after everything that had happened. There was no way all of this was going to be for nothing.

Kat knew Kirsty wouldn't be the same without her sidekick Rachel around, and Kat was the only person in the world who knew with absolute certainty that Rachel would never be back.

She hadn't taken her eyes off Kirsty for most of the morning so far, and Kirsty hadn't looked her usual assured self. Maybe she knew something had happened to her horrible friend?

Kirsty walked by Kat's desk, heading for the toilets.

Kat dropped what she was doing and followed.

She entered the ladies' toilet and waited at the sinks. Kirsty was in one of the cubicles. Was it the same one Kat had been locked in? She couldn't remember. After a couple of minutes, the cubicle door opened and out came Kat's tormentor. The person who had somehow made Rachel come to her flat and kill her cat. Kat pretended to wash her hands.

Kat realised she had no idea what the hell she was doing in the toilet. She had bunched her fists in anticipation of seeing Kirsty, but there was no way she was going to do anything. For one thing, if there was some sort of fight or confrontation, then it would come out when the police investigated Rachel's disappearance. It wouldn't look good. Kat had to play it cool, even if she was boiling inside. Being so close to the girl who had made her life a living hell for the past six months and not being able to do anything was hugely frustrating, yet Kat had to keep her head.

'Hi, Kirsty. How are you?' Kat said with a smile and a new-found confidence.

Kirsty was taken aback; Kat had never initiated a conversation between the two of them before.

'Eh, I'm fine,' Kirsty replied warily. 'How are you?'

'I'm good, thanks,' Kat said before leaving a stunned Kirsty standing in the toilet.

Kat let out a large breath when she got into the corridor. She needed to plan what she should do. That could have gone horribly wrong. She moved away from the toilets so she wouldn't bump into Kirsty again. Kat knew what she had done was stupid beyond belief. She should have been staying out of Kirsty's way, yet she had actually sought her out.

Kat's phone buzzed in her bag as she made her way out of the office. She lifted it out. It was a number she didn't recognise so she let it go to voicemail. She could do without pests on the phone just now. Whoever it was had left a message though. Kat put the phone to her ear and listened.

'Miss Matthews, this is PC Thomas McFarlane. I've been dealing with your stolen car report and I've got good news and bad news. Good news: I've located your vehicle. Bad news: I'm afraid to say that the car's been burnt to a cinder. Can you contact me at the station or call me back on…'

35

Kat knew she had to deal with her 'stolen' car in a way that wouldn't arouse any suspicion. She was very surprised, not to say disappointed, that the Mini had been found so quickly. All she could do was pray that any evidence which might have been left had been thoroughly destroyed by the fire. Also, Kat reasoned that the police wouldn't actively be searching the car for clues. As yet, they didn't know anything untoward had occurred. They certainly wouldn't be linking the car to any suspicious deaths.

Kat returned the phone call from the young-sounding PC and arranged to go in and see him. There was no point putting it off, so she made her way from work to the police station immediately after her shift. She entered the station and tried not to look as shifty and nervous as she felt. She was sweating profusely. A lot rested on how this meeting went. She had got away with the CCTV missing everything, but if they found any incriminating evidence in the car it could see all of this come to an abrupt end.

After giving her details at the front desk, she waited for PC McFarlane to arrive. She tried to calm herself down. This was nothing to worry about. It was merely a formality, she tried to reassure herself.

PC Thomas McFarlane appeared after twenty minutes or so of nervous waiting. He was at least six foot five and had a shock of ginger hair and the beginnings of a ginger beard, although Kat wasn't sure he was actually old enough to grow one. He looked as if he was on work experience from school.

'Miss Matthews, thanks for coming down. If you'd like to take a seat in here, we can get started.'

Kat was delighted that such a junior officer had been assigned to her missing car. She followed the tall policeman into a small room just off the reception area.

'Take a seat. Terrible business about your car. We found your vehicle on some waste ground in the Maryhill area of the city. I'm sorry to say that someone did a right number on it – when we found the vehicle it was burnt to a cinder.' He obviously liked that analogy; he'd used it twice now. 'There was nothing in the car that could be saved – it's a complete write-off.'

Kat tried to hide her pleasure at this news; she feared the heavy rain might have put the fire out before all of the damage could be done, leaving traces of clothing or DNA.

'There wasn't even anything worth stealing in the car,' Kat said. A nice touch, she thought.

'I'm afraid it happens. Probably just youngsters taking it for a joyride and then getting rid of the evidence. We've had an unfortunately high number of these incidents over the past couple of months.'

The police had, quite reasonably, assumed the car had been stolen and burnt out by joyriders. The young PC had told Kat there was nothing else that they could do and as far as they were concerned that was that. Case closed.

This was music to Kat's ears.

36

She started a conversation with me. The fat cow started a conversation. With me. I couldn't believe it. Who the fuck does she think she is? The fat rodent cornering me in the fuckin toilets like that. I'm going to have to talk to my dad about this. This can't be allowed to go on.

Rachel's still in the huff. She's still not came into work, and she's still not text me back. She's not even been on Snapchat or Insta. I'll need to see her because she's becoming a problem I can do without. Wait til I tell her that the fat bitch spoke to me. She'll go nuts.

All I know is that it's full steam ahead with the plan. We're going to have to get our arse in gear now and just make it happen. Fat Kat's not going to be speaking to me again in a hurry – not when she finds out what we've got planned for her.

37

Kat was pleased that her trip to the police station had turned out well and hadn't resulted in her arrest for murder. In the back of her mind she was convinced they would have found something incriminating in the remnants of the Mini, but her fears had been unfounded. The car shouldn't cause her any more problems. Now, Kat had to try to list all of the other ways in which she was vulnerable and think about what might lead to her getting caught or even implicated in Rachel's death.

She had tried to figure out how the police would approach their investigation when it inevitably started. She didn't have any friends who were in the police or any inside knowledge whatsoever. She was also sure not to google anything that would look bad for her at a later date. She certainly wasn't going to google 'how to get away with murder' or anything to do with forensics. There had been recent cases on the news which had found the defendant guilty after finding their ill-advised and frankly ridiculous internet searches.

The only information Kat had about police procedures was gleaned from years of watching badly acted detective dramas on television and reading the odd bit of crime fiction. Hopefully they were at least a little realistic. Once the body was discovered, and Kat hoped that would be a long time hence, she knew the police would look at a timeline of events from when Rachel was last seen alive and well. That would have been around 6 p.m. in the office – although she left before then, didn't she? Kat tried to remember. She herself left at 6 p.m. and she was pretty sure Rachel had left some time before. Then she had confronted Kat in the car park, which had led to the fatal incident. Rachel didn't drive though. Kat knew she got the bus in – she was constantly moaning about public transport and used it as an excuse for the multiple times she was late. So had Rachel just gone down to the car park to confront and attack Kat? It was certainly looking that way. Kat knew the police would speak to her and all of her colleagues eventually. She wanted to get it clear in her mind what she would say. And what she wouldn't.

She had already checked to see if the CCTV had captured the two of them in the car park. Her luck had held in that regard. Where else would the cameras have caught sight of Rachel? In work, there were no cameras in the lift. It had been brought up many times before as a possible issue, but the managers had insisted the lift would be replaced soon and cameras installed then. The last sighting of Rachel would have been in the corridor when she left the office, and who knew how long the tapes or digital images from that camera were kept? Kat was reasonably sure the CCTV would not implicate her, though luck would have to play its part again. Kat didn't like leaving her fate to such things, but there was nothing she could do about it. The CCTV might show Kat going back out of the lift and heading to the cleaner's cupboard, but that didn't prove anything, did it? Kat wasn't even sure there was a camera covering the cupboard. She hoped not. There was no way she could check through every camera in the bank or surrounding areas. The only way Kat thought she could potentially get caught was through Rachel's phone, and she was going to deal with that imminently.

Kat had left the police station and made her way onto Union Street, where she would get a bus to visit her mother in the nursing home. It was busy with commuters making their way home after work.

Before Kat boarded the bus, she set out to get rid of any trace of her name from the handset. She deleted her number, which had been lovingly entered as 'Fat Kat'. She erased the numerous nasty messages which had been sent to her and deleted the conversation between Kirsty and Rachel which talked at length about the bullying, then erased the WhatsApp application. She was sure to be mentioned on that and she wasn't really too sure how to use it. Kat knew the police could probably retrieve the deleted items, but it was all she could do. She could destroy the phone, but she had ideas forming that absolutely needed the device.

Kat realised as she was deleting all these items that she hadn't checked the phone's camera roll yet. She had been too busy with the multitude of juicy messages. She swiped through numerous pouting selfies of Rachel then nearly vomited up her lunch. Kat was stunned. She zoomed into the photo. There was no doubt about it: Rachel was posing with Kirsty and an older woman who was surely her mother and what looked like her father or stepfather. The horrifying thing was though…

It was Stephen. Kat's ex-husband.

Ste was Stephen.

38

How could she have been so stupid?

Ste was Stephen. Kat's ex-husband.

The whole sorry situation slowly came together in Kat's mind. It had been staring her in the face the whole time. That no-good scumbag was behind all of this.

Stephen had shacked up with Rachel's mother. And Kirsty was involved somehow. Were Rachel and Kirsty sisters? Or stepsisters? Kat looked through the photos some more. There were various happy family snaps of Rachel with her mum, Rachel with Kirsty, Rachel with her dogs and Rachel with her stepdad/lover Ste – or as Kat knew him, Stephen.

The bullying by Rachel and Kirsty made a little more sense now. They were being led by Stephen. He had instigated all of this. But to what end? What were they hoping to achieve? Was this purely to get back at her for chucking him out all those years ago? Were they just trying to make her life a misery as some sort of weird revenge?

Kat flicked through some more photos. She was completely oblivious to the hustle and bustle of the busy street around her as she stood at the bus stop. A set showed Stephen's birthday and one of them had a caption: 'Kirsty and her lovely dad'.

That confirmed it. Kirsty was Stephen's daughter. Kat stared at the image on screen. She couldn't believe this. She couldn't take it all in.

'You alright, love?' an elderly man asked Kat. His voice immediately brought her back to the present. She had been completely lost in the phone and had blanked out her surroundings. The bus stops on Union Street were extremely busy and the old man must have noticed Kat engrossed in the mobile with a shocked look on her face. Her mouth was hanging open as she skimmed through the photo album.

'I'm fine, thanks,' Kat said. She really was anything but fine.

'You don't look fine,' the old man continued. 'You look like you've seen a bloody ghost.'

'Honestly, I'm good,' Kat replied. The old man didn't know how right he was. Kat smiled politely at him and moved off to another bus stop. She didn't want to be rude, but she really wasn't in the mood for any conversation. Not after seeing all of this. She settled in at another bus stop and tried to think.

Kat couldn't have known Kirsty was Stephen's daughter and Rachel his stepdaughter. She had no reason to suspect that all of the bullying stemmed from Stephen. How could she have known? She tried to piece it all together.

The same man who had run for the hills when Kat was pregnant with Paul had a daughter of his own. The same man who had come back three times yet still didn't want anything to do with his own son had a daughter. The same scumbag who hadn't contributed whatsoever to his upbringing had a daughter! And that same daughter had made Kat's life a complete and utter misery. Kat was furious now.

It all fell into place. The whole sordid truth. Rachel and Kirsty were stepsisters and Stephen had wormed his way into their lives. He was seeing Rachel's mum and he was having an affair with Rachel, his stepdaughter. Abusing his position in the family. A heavily messed-up family. The two girls were bullying Kat because Stephen must have been filling their heads with all sorts of nonsense. Rachel had paid the price with her life. It was senseless. She had died because of Stephen and his twisted lies and stories.

Kat now had a plan forming in her head. Rachel's body might be found soon… and Stephen would be getting the blame.

Kat was damn sure of that.

39

Kat had never felt anger like this before in her entire life. The initial shock of seeing Stephen's photo on Rachel's phone had turned to red-hot anger. She couldn't believe everything had happened because of him. Somehow though, Kat felt as if she should have known. Most of the problems in her life seemed to have stemmed from him in one way or another. Kat now had a clear focus as to what to do next. She was going to try to frame Stephen for Rachel's murder and hopefully implicate his evil daughter Kirsty for good measure. It was the least the two of them deserved.

The photos and messages in Rachel's phone made it clear to anyone that she was having an illicit affair with her own stepfather. There was no way you could look at the texts and not come to that conclusion. Kat was going to help the police zone in on a prime suspect when they opened up their missing-person or murder enquiry.

Still standing at the bus stop, she opened up the notes section of Rachel's phone and started writing, trying to imitate Rachel's language and style.

It's getting too real now. Ste shouldn't be doing what he's doing with me. I'm scared to stop though – he's already threatened me and I think the next time he might go too far. I know his temper is real bad. I don't want to be on the end of it again. I'll need to try and get away. It's the only option. Ste will kill me otherwise. Kirsty as well. The two of them are a horrible pair. I wish they'd never come into my life.

Kat saved the note. The police would surely forensically examine the phone and when they did eventually see the note, it would help them along. It would plant the seed in their heads that Stephen and Kirsty could have been involved in her disappearance and subsequently her murder, once they had recovered a body. It showed that they were working together as a team. The note plus all of the messages and photos were damning evidence. Kat just hoped the officers investigating would see it that way.

Kat gave the phone a good wipe down with a disinfectant wipe; she tried to eliminate all of her fingerprints. No one seemed to be paying her a blind bit of attention. Everyone was either too busy on their phones or eagerly looking for the bus that would take them home. She placed a wipe on top of the handset and turned the phone off. She then placed it in a small plastic zip bag and slipped it into the inside pocket of her jacket. She would get rid of it tonight, on her way back from the care home.

Kat knew exactly where she was going to put the phone.

40

Even with all that was going on, Kat still had to look in on her mother. Getting away with murder could wait for an hour or two, and Kat was in dire need of a break. Plus, she was killing time before she could get rid of Rachel's phone under the cover of darkness.

Kat entered her mother's room to find Maureen in her usual chair staring at the television. She was watching *Emmerdale*. She loved her soaps and spent hours each day watching them. It pleased her seeing the misery and chaos heaped upon the characters. She said it was an escape from her own mundane existence stuck in the care home, but Kat knew that she actually quite liked it here. There was always something going on for her mother to gossip about.

Maureen turned to see who had entered.

'Mum, you found your teeth!' Kat said.

'Aye, great. Your wee mum's got teeth again. Get the bunting out. Never mind about everything else they've stolen from me.'

'Don't be silly, Mum; no one's stealing anything from you.'

'What? I'm telling ye, that Irene Jenkins is stealing left, right and centre. She'll steal the eyes from your heed given half a chance.'

Kat tried not to laugh and took a seat across from her mother. They sat in silence until an advert break in her programme. Kat knew better than to interrupt her mother's soaps.

'How's thing's at that work of yours?' Maureen asked.

'Things are fine. I'm going for a promotion actually. I don't hold out much hope, but even applying is a step in the right direction.'

'About bloody time you should be getting promoted. I never raised no meek mouse – you should be running that place by now.'

'Did you hear Paul and Charlotte's good news?' Kat asked, trying to change the subject.

'Aye, Paul phoned me a few times about it. I don't think he knows what he's let himself in for. He thinks it's all going to be sunshine and light,' Maureen said. Paul phoning her mother was news to Kat.

Kat turned the conversation onto another much riskier topic – her ex-husband Stephen. She couldn't get him and all that had gone on out of her mind.

'I came across Stephen earlier. Did you ever notice anything dodgy about him?'

'Dodgy? Everything about that no-good arsehole was dodgy. I told you at the beginning, I could see it clear as day. Your father could see it and he was half blind, but you just wouldn't take a telling.'

'I think he's up to his old tricks again.'

'Leopards don't change their spots – is that not what they say? What's the piece of shite up to now?' Kat's mother certainly had a way with words.

'I'm not so sure, but I saw him with a younger woman. A much younger woman.' Kat couldn't say she had been reading the messages and looking at the photos on his dead stepdaughter's phone. A dead stepdaughter who he had been having an affair with.

'He always did like them young. You should have chinned him for all the money he took from you or for not paying a single penny to Paul. Steer well clear of him, Katherine. The last thing you want is that loser back in your life. Paul would never forgive you if you took him back again.'

'There's no chance of that. Believe me.' Kat decided to keep her counsel – if she told her mum about Stephen's latest antics it would be around the nursing home in ten minutes. She needed to keep the gruesome details to herself.

'You need to put that arsehole out of that heed of yours. He was a wrong'un back then and I'd bet my last pound that he's still a wrong'un just now.' Maureen, as usual, was right on the money.

'I will, Mum – thanks.'

'Are you eating? You look like you're losing weight,' Maureen said, looking Kat up and down.

'Yes, I'm eating. I've been trying to lose a bit of weight though, so thank you.'

'I don't like it. Get eating again. I canny be having you getting too skinny.'

'Okay, Mum,' Kat said. 'Do you need me to get you anything?'

'No, no, I'm braw,' Maureen said. Kat could see that another one of her mother's shows was starting.

'I'll let you know how I get on at work; hopefully I'll have some good news for a change,' Kat said before the show started.

'You do that. Now get out of the bloody way of that telly – *EastEnders* is coming on.'

41

Kat had met Stephen when they were teenagers. It had been her first proper relationship and it had scarred her for life. He was loving and kind for the first few years – they'd always had a good laugh at the start. Then Kat had fallen pregnant and everything changed. Stephen's mask had well and truly slipped.

The laughs stopped; Stephen was no longer loving and kind. It was like the flick of a switch. He completely changed, and he started treating Kat as if she was something he'd found on the sole of his shoe. It all came to a head one night when Kat, heavily pregnant, had come home early from work. She had been feeling terrible, and her situation wasn't improved when she walked in on Stephen in an intimate embrace with their teenage neighbour. It turned out he had been 'intimately embracing' everything that moved. He tried to wriggle his way out of it with some terrible excuses, but Kat was not one for second chances back then – she had thrown him out. The neighbour had only been about sixteen or seventeen. What was it her mother had said? He always liked them young?

Kat hadn't seen Stephen for a few years after that. Then, out of the blue, he had appeared at her door with some tall tale or other, and Kat foolishly had been taken in. He had changed; he was a different person. He was sorry for all of the pain and hurt he had caused. He wanted to get to know his son. 'Just give me a chance,' he had pleaded. He had lasted three weeks before his true colours were revealed and he had been shown the door again.

When Paul was sixteen and a troublesome teenager, Stephen had resurfaced again and Kat ridiculously had succumbed to his charms once more. She had made a huge error of judgement. She couldn't believe she had been taken for a fool yet again when he'd showed up at her door in need of help and she had taken him in. Paul had been furious. They hadn't spoken for months because of it, and it had nearly destroyed their relationship irrevocably. Kat's mother and father weren't best pleased either, and Kat felt it had played a part in her father's health deteriorating. Thankfully, it hadn't taken Stephen long to mess it all up. He had been stealing money from her, and Kat was convinced he'd been playing away again, so she had thrown him out of her life forever this time. Apart from receiving bills in his name, she hadn't heard from or come across Stephen for several years until this sorry mess had started.

Stephen was fifty-one years old now and Rachel was only late teens or early twenties – and his stepdaughter. How long had it been going on? It was wrong on so many levels. Stephen was going to pay for this particular indiscretion. In fact, after all the years of hurt and pain, he deserved everything that was coming to him.

Kat hadn't got around to getting a new car yet so she was stuck with public transport. She left the nursing home and got on a bus heading for the city centre. She hoped there would be no reason for the police to check the bus's CCTV images, as there was nothing she could do to avoid them. She exited the bus when it arrived in the bustling city centre and headed to St Enoch subway station. She still had a short yet vital journey to make.

Kat had wiped Rachel's phone down several times over the past few days. She had given it one last clean before she left the care home and had slipped it into the little zip bag again. She really should have worn gloves every time she used it, but this would have to do. She had tried to erase any mention of herself, of her cat or anything remotely linked to the bullying. She hoped this would work.

Kat left the subway at St George's Cross and made her way to her intended destination… the house Stephen shared with Kirsty, Rachel and her mum.

42

Kat had walked past the house three or four times. She was trying to make absolutely sure that this was the right place. She was certain it was. She had found the address via Rachel's phone and the internet. She had been on street maps via Rachel's phone to scope it out, and now she stood on the very street watching and waiting. There were some trees across the road from the house and Kat waited patiently underneath them, hoping she wouldn't look too dodgy if she was seen. The lighting wasn't great, which helped hide her from view. Thankfully, the rain had abated for now, although there were large, ominous dark clouds in the night sky.

Kat knew from the brutal messages she had read that some of Rachel and Stephen's secret trysts had taken place in his garden shed. What a truly romantic bastard he was. He obviously hadn't changed one bit over the years. Kat had spotted the small wooden construction at the back of the house in the overgrown garden. Stephen never had been a keen gardener.

Kat fixed her leather gloves on and felt inside her jacket for the phone. There were still lights on in the house, but she couldn't wait all night – she needed to get out of there before someone noticed her loitering around and confronted her – or worse, phoned the police. She gathered up the required courage and made her move. She walked around to the side of the house and quickly bypassed the door. The garden was just about in darkness. Kat pulled a screwdriver from her jacket and moved to the rickety shed.

Kat prised open the flimsy lock with the screwdriver – it gave way easily. She was in. The shed smelled of petrol and grass. It wasn't exactly a place you would want to spend time in. It had an old ragged sofa bed at the far end, in between all sorts of golf clubs and gardening implements that evidently hadn't been used for years. Kat shuddered at what had gone on in this place.

She lifted the phone out of the plastic zip bag and turned the device back on.

She pushed the phone down the side of the tattered and heavily stained couch bed. The battery still had a fair bit of life left. Kat hoped the police could track the phone and locate it in the shed – it would look bad for Stephen and further enhance his credentials as the main suspect when it was found. They could even test the stains on the couch.

Kat froze. She heard something – someone had appeared from the house. They were talking in hushed tones. For a horrible second, Kat thought she had been seen.

They were talking on the phone. Kat peered out through the crack in the door. It was Stephen. He was animated as he spoke into his mobile. Kat's heart was racing. If he walked over to the shed, she was done for. He would notice it was open. She held her breath.

Stephen walked closer to the shed.

He was going to find her. Kat looked around the shed for a hiding place. There was nowhere she could go without making all sorts of noise. She picked up a golf club that was lying on the floor, gripped it tightly and watched.

Stephen paced up and down the garden, still talking into the phone. Kat couldn't quite make out what he was saying but it seemed to be an important call. She stood completely still, terrified he would open the shed door.

She gripped the golf club tighter still.

'What you doing out there, Ste?' someone shouted from the house. It must have been his wife, Rachel's mother.

Stephen quickly ended his phone call.

'I'm just coming, honey,' he shouted. He looked shifty, then he turned and looked right at Kat. Or at least that's what it felt like. He moved closer to the shed. Kat braced herself and gripped the club.

'Stephen!' the shout came again. More insistent this time. Stephen turned on his heel and made his way back inside.

Kat breathed a huge sigh of relief.

That had been far too close for comfort.

Kat, in a cold sweat, reached into her jacket and came out with a small vial. A small vial which contained some of Rachel's blood. Kat had the idea when she was cleaning up the bloodstains in the car and found to her surprise that some of it was still wet – she'd thought it might come in useful somehow. It had been another moment of madness, but now she was going to use it to her advantage. She was going to put the final nail in Stephen's coffin and seal his guilt in the eyes of the police. Kat dropped a few spots of blood onto the couch and on the floor of the shed. She smeared a little on the door. The police would almost certainly be forensically searching the shed soon, and when they found drops of Rachel's blood it would be curtains for Stephen. Kat couldn't believe she could be so callous. It was so cold and calculating, and so out of character.

Kat used up the blood and closed the vial, slipping it back into her jacket pocket. She waited another minute until she was certain the coast was clear and then exited the shed. She tried to press the lock back into place and closed the door. Unless you were looking for it, there didn't look like any sign of a forced entry.

Who had Kat become? Breaking and entering whilst framing someone with a vial of a dead girl's blood? Well, she supposed after murder it was a minor crime.

Kat had reasoned that sooner or later the police would search the shed and when the phone was found they would read all of the messages between stepfather and daughter. The blood would cement his guilt. Then it was up to the creep to try to worm his way out of it.

The messages, photos and blood spots were damning evidence. Kat was sure that Stephen would be looked upon as a suspect. He *had* to be looked at as a suspect.

Kat's nerves were shredded after the close encounter with her ex. She silently moved back out of the garden and past the door, praying no one would see her.

Back out in the street, Kat let out another huge sigh of relief and headed for home.

Her nerves may have been completely shot but Kat let another smile cross her lips. Another part of her plan had been successfully completed.

43

Rachel better not ruin this for me and Dad. She's being an attention-seeking little cow. She needs to get back right now before someone phones the polis.

We know the fat bitch has money stashed away – we just need to get our hands on it and then it's game over. I've told Dad we need to make a move now, but he wants to wait, make her suffer some more. He always wants her to suffer more.

I can't wait until it's done and she knows what's happened. We can get away from this shithole and stop pretending to play happy families with these fucking clowns. My lovely stepmummy Laura will be out of my life forever and I'll never have to set eyes on her daft daughter ever again either. I know they didn't even want me moving in with them in the first place.

It's not like we don't deserve it. Me and Dad. Dad told me that the fat bitch didn't want anything to do with me. She even talked about putting me up for adoption. Adoption! She hasn't paid one penny to me or Dad through my whole life. Bet she hasn't even wondered what the hell happened to me. How I turned out. She just left Dad to struggle on and got on with her life. Fat, selfish bitch.

I can't wait to see her face when she finds out the truth.

44

The alarm on Kat's bedside table sounded at 7 a.m. but she was already wide awake. Had been for hours. She hadn't been sleeping well since Rachel died. A few snatched hours here and there had been her lot. Several times now she had closed her eyes and been on the verge of sleep when the image of Rachel covered in flames startled her back awake with a jolt. Once, Kat was sure it was an image of Kirsty in the flames.

She turned on the radio for the hourly news as she had done throughout the night. There had been nothing so far about the case, but this morning's bulletin was different and much more interesting.

'Police are becoming increasingly concerned over the disappearance of Glasgow woman Rachel Strang. The nineteen-year-old hasn't been seen for three days now, and family and friends say this is extremely out of character. Miss Strang's fiancé Jason Thomson is pleading for her safe return.'

'Rachel, I just want to know you're okay. Contact me or your mum – we're going out of our minds here.'

'Anyone who has any information about Miss Strang's whereabouts is urged to get in contact with Police Scotland. More details and a photo of Rachel can be found on our website…'

Kat knew it was only a matter of time before Rachel's disappearance made the news. She had expected it. She was young. She was popular. It was inevitable. It was still a strange experience hearing her name on the news though. Kat was hugely relieved that she had managed to get rid of the phone before the news broke. It pleased her that the phone and blood would now implicate Stephen.

The news bulletin was a stark reminder that this was all very real. It had happened. Kat sat on her bed and felt a little numb. She hadn't expected to hear Rachel's fiancé speak. She had heard his voice on Rachel's phone when he'd left a voicemail. He would be filled with false hope at the moment. So would her mother. Little did they know it was only a matter of time before a murder enquiry was launched.

Kat opened her phone and navigated to the radio station's website, clicked news and looked at what was their top story. The smiling photo of Rachel made her look almost angelic. It was not the person Kat recognised. Even though the news report had said more details were available on their website, there didn't appear to be a great deal of further information. The photo and physical description, plus a mention of her workplace were the only new details.

However, Kat couldn't help feeling pangs of guilt. She was to blame for so much hurt and pain that was to come for Rachel's family. Although it had been an accident. A terrible bloody accident. If the little witch hadn't attacked her in the car park then none of this would have happened. When she thought about it – and if she was completely honest with herself – she was only feeling sorry for Rachel's mother. Then again, it was the mother who had raised such a horrible, spiteful little bitch and had taken in the complete and utter arsehole that was Stephen. Maybe she was partly to blame as well? Kat's thoughts were muddled – she really needed to get a good night's sleep.

Rachel's mother didn't know it yet but she was in for some real shocks. She may have felt despair and helplessness just now when she thought her daughter was only missing, but it was nothing to what she would experience in the near future.

Her daughter had been killed, albeit accidently. Her daughter had been disposed of in a cold and calculated manner, though there was nothing accidental about that. And to top it all off, her husband had been screwing said daughter behind her back for God knows how long. It would be a lot for anyone to take.

The fiancé Jason wouldn't be too chuffed either when he found out his soon-to-be-wife had been cheating on him with at least two others behind his back. His temper would be stretched to its limits.

Maybe she should let Jason know exactly what had been going on. Maybe she should let them all know what Rachel and Stephen had been up to.

Kat smiled. She should let them all know.

45

'Do you know how many calories are in those?' DI Alan Prentice said. He was watching his colleague demolish his second roll and potato scone of the day.

'I'm guessing by the look on your face that it's a fair number… but do you know what, Al? I couldn't care less, mate. I'm happy,' DS Donaldson said as he licked more tomato sauce from his fingers. He genuinely did look happy with himself.

Prentice shook his head. He knew there was no talking to Donaldson. He was never going to embrace the healthy lifestyle he himself loved so much.

Donaldson was clinically obese, but he didn't seem to mind. Prentice was a fitness fanatic. The pair of them made an unlikely but ultimately winning team. They had worked together for only a few months, but they played to each other's strengths.

Prentice and Donaldson had been given the task of tracking down a missing girl. DCI Brannigan was leading the team, but both Prentice and Donaldson knew that meant they would be doing most of the work. Brannigan liked to think he was hands-on, however, more often than not he let his team get on with it, only swooping in when the credit was being dished out.

Both detectives knew only too well that the first few days in a missing-person enquiry were crucial. They both worked for the Major Investigations Unit and they had taken the case from the local police when it appeared the girl could be in serious danger. This, as you can imagine, didn't make them too popular with the local detectives who had to hand over the case.

The MIU wouldn't normally be called in so early in a missing-person enquiry. However, it had emerged during initial enquires that the missing girl was engaged to the nephew of one of Glasgow's oldest and most prolific gangsters – a genuinely horrible chap by the name of Archie Thomson. Those above Prentice wanted to make sure there was no link to organised crime in the poor girl's disappearance. It certainly made the case more intriguing. Many of Police Scotland's finest had tried to make something stick to Archie Thomson over the years but without success.

Rachel Strang was the missing girl's name. Nineteen years old. They had already been to the family home along with a family liaison officer. Nothing had seemed out of the ordinary, apart from the fact she had gone AWOL. The mother had reported her missing and she was frantic, as was to be expected. The father, or stepfather as he'd informed them, had seemed concerned. They said Rachel had never gone missing before, plus they had always kept in contact via phone or social media. It was very much out of character for her. This in itself had drawn Rachel's mother, Laura, to the conclusion that something untoward had happened to her daughter. Prentice tended to agree. Donaldson was absolutely certain of it.

Prentice enjoyed the challenges his work brought. He knew missing-person cases were hard to solve, and often many of the cases evolved into murder enquiries. He wasn't sure which way this one would go, but if he were to play the percentages, he would hazard a guess that at this point in the enquiry there was a fifty per cent chance of the girl being found alive and well. Donaldson wouldn't even entertain such a thought. He was very much of the opinion that the girl had come to grievous harm.

Family and friends is where Prentice always started these investigations. More often than not, the missing person had confided to someone close about what they planned to do. Or a close person was responsible for something nasty happening to them. Either way, it normally involved someone they knew. Of course, some missing people did not want to be found but, on the face of it, this didn't seem to be the case here. Prentice knew, especially with younger folk, that social media and mobile phones played key roles in any enquiry. He had already instructed some of his guys to focus on her accounts and try to track down her phone. He wanted to know the last time her phone had been used and, if possible, where. He wanted to know everything about her social-media usage. He was good at his job and would leave no stone unturned in finding the young girl. Hopefully she would turn up unharmed.

The case would undoubtedly receive good media attention and Prentice had been instructed by DCI Brannigan to make the best use of it and to let him know when he was needed to go on camera. Prentice was not to 'let them down' or 'make the force look bad' after a string of cases which had resulted in adverse publicity. Trust in Police Scotland was at an all-time low according to the media, but then again when was that not the case?

46

Kat arrived at work to find the place swarming with police. They were gathered outside the bank on Bothwell Street, inside at the front lobby handing out leaflets with Rachel's photo on it and in the office where both Kat and Rachel worked. Kat took one of the proffered sheets and headed up the stairs. It wasn't a shock seeing the police at the bank – she had expected them to come. However, the sheer number of officers was surprising. All you read about was cutbacks in the police force, yet there must have been around thirty officers at the bank. This showed how seriously they were taking Rachel's disappearance. They were being organised by two men in suits. They were an odd-looking couple. One was very tall and looked like he could be a male model, with an expensive suit and designer stubble. The other was smaller in height but hugely overweight, with what looked like egg stains on his garish tie.

Kat wasn't as nervous as she ought to have been in this situation, which felt strange. She had to admit to herself that her life was a hell of a lot better without Rachel in it, and it would be even better still if Kirsty had suffered the same fate. If Kirsty went away for killing or helping Stephen to kill Rachel then Kat would be delighted. It would kill two birds with one stone, so to speak.

Kat entered her office, where yet more police were gathered. She was relieved she had got rid of Rachel's phone. It would have made things very stressful indeed if she was still carrying that about.

After a while Tony gathered the team together. This was a rare occurrence indeed; he normally just sat alone in his office surfing the internet. By the look of his puffy red eyes he had been crying. He looked frantic. His eyes were darting around the room as he spoke.

'Right, folks, listen up. The police are going to have a word with all of us. They've set up in the meeting room. If you know anything about where Rachel is then you need to tell them. You need to. Anything. Any information at all will help. We all just want her back,' Tony said, sniffing back yet more tears. Many of the staff looked perplexed as to why Tony was so upset. Kat knew the reason all too well.

Kat watched throughout the morning as some of her colleagues went in to be questioned. The whole office was alive with chatter about Rachel. The gossips were having a field day. Where was she? What had happened to her? What was the deal with Tony crying?

Kat's turn came just after her morning break. The two police officers welcomed her into the room which was used for team meetings on the odd occasion they actually took place. She closed the door behind her and sat across from them. Kat didn't feel nervous; she wasn't sweating. She seemed, if anything, a little numb to the whole situation. She had known the police would probably want to speak to her and all of her colleagues at some point, and she'd played this scenario through many times in her head over the past few days. What she should say. What she shouldn't say. How she should act.

'As you know, we're here today about the disappearance of Rachel Strang. We're trying to gather as much detail as possible about her movements. When was the last time you saw Rachel?' the female officer asked. She was smartly dressed and had introduced herself. Kat couldn't recall if it was her first or last name that was Kelly. The bald male officer had a notepad at the ready for any nuggets of information. His name was Angus, and again Kat wasn't sure if this was a Christian or surname.

Kat focused on the question. She couldn't very well say, 'The last time I saw Rachel, I was setting her on fire to dispose of any evidence because unfortunately we had a struggle in the car park and she died.' She composed herself and answered sensibly.

'I think it would have been Monday in the office.'

'Did you notice anything off about Rachel or anything unusual?' Kelly said.

'To be honest, me and Rachel aren't really that friendly – I don't really speak to her much at all. You know how it is, young girl like that, she probably doesn't have much in common with someone like me. So no I didn't really notice anything, but then again I wouldn't really have been looking,' Kat said. She was rambling on a bit. She had made sure to use the present tense when talking about Rachel.

'Have you any idea what might have happened to her or if anyone had any grievance against Miss Strang?' the male officer, Angus, asked. He looked thoroughly bored. He had sat through ten or so of these meetings already today so who could blame him.

'I don't have a clue. I wish I could be more help, I really do, but the first I heard about all of this was on the news this morning. It was a shock, I can tell you. I just hope she's back soon.'

This seemed to satisfy both officers, although they looked a little downtrodden with the news that yet another interview wasn't going to glean them any useful information.

'If you can think of anything further then please get in touch with us,' Kelly said hopefully.

'I've got the number on the leaflet here, so I'll be in touch if I can offer any help,' Kat replied.

The two officers seemed to have exhausted their line of questioning. It had been exactly as Kat expected. There was no reason for them to be asking Kat much about Rachel – as far as they were concerned they were work colleagues who hadn't had much to do with each other. Further down the line though, there might be some harder or more awkward questions to answer.

Kat was on her way out of the meeting room when something struck her. She turned with the door slightly ajar.

'Why is Tony so upset about Rachel going missing? I mean, we all want her found but why is he in tears? Does he know something we don't?' Kat said.

The two officers looked at Kat and considered what she had said. It seemed like new information to them. They looked interested for the first time since the meeting began.

'Thanks for your help, Miss Matthews.' the male officer said.

'No problem. No problem at all,' Kat said, leaving the room.

47

Kat got home earlier than usual from work. She didn't have a dead girl's phone to dissect in a dodgy cafe tonight, and she hadn't stayed on later to make up the rest of the time she owed. She turned on the television for the STV news at 6 p.m. Kat knew with certainty that Rachel would be on it. It was a given after seeing first-hand the sheer number of police assigned to find her. However, she had no idea Rachel would be the top story. The news anchor gave a brief synopsis of the events so far and then handed over to a young female reporter who was standing outside Rachel's house with a forced look of concern on her face. The house with the shed in the garden where Kat had hidden the phone. The house where Rachel had stayed with her mother, stepfather and stepsister. It felt surreal watching the place on the news. Kat listened intently to the report.

'What started out as a missing-person enquiry has quickly evolved into something far more sinister it would seem today. Police sources have told us that they are extremely concerned about the whereabouts and well-being of nineteen-year-old Rachel Strang, who hasn't been seen for several days now. Police are saying tonight that this is highly unusual for the teenager who is very sociable and has never been out of contact with her friends and family for any period of time.

'Police have today been at Rachel's workplace in Glasgow city centre and have spent a considerable period of time at the family home behind me, where forensic officers have been coming and going all day. The family car has also been taken away for testing. Now, this in itself doesn't mean that Rachel has come to any harm; however, it is a very concerning time for all who know her. Anyone who has any information about Rachel's whereabouts is urged to get in contact with Police Scotland on the number on screen now. Also, the police are asking if anyone has any dash-cam footage from the St George's Cross area of the city that might show Rachel can they get in touch? Back to you in the studio, John.'

In the background you could clearly see forensic officers in their white suits coming and going. They had erected a blue tent at the side of the front door. They were sure to look in the shed and find the phone. The fact they had taken away the family car for testing also indicated that the police knew Rachel was dead – and that family members might be involved. Kat wasn't expecting reporters to be camped outside the house. Not yet. No body had been found, but it showed that the police and media were taking the case very seriously indeed.

Kat rewound the report and watched it again.

48

'I saw your work on the telly, Katherine,' Maureen Matthews said. 'Some lassie's gone missing?' Kat wasn't even in the door yet.

'Yeah, a girl called Rachel Strang. Been missing for a while now,' Kat said. She was already on the back foot; she hadn't expected her mother to quiz her on this. However, Rachel had been on every news report and was on the front page of most newspapers. The media had been camped outside her house and outside the bank for a couple of days now.

'How come you never mentioned it and I had to hear about it on the bloody news like every other Tom, Dick and Harry?'

'I didn't think it was that interesting to be honest—'

'Not that interesting? What's the point of having my only daughter working in the very place a girl goes missing and she doesn't even tell her old mum about it? I had to hear it off that bloody Lena McPherson.'

'Sorry, Mum; I should have mentioned it. Anyway—'

'I take it you don't like her?'

'What? No, I—'

'Your old mum's hit the nail on the head, hasn't she? I can see it on your face – you hated her. What was she like? Do you think she's come to a sticky end?' Maureen said.

This was worse than the police interrogation. Maureen was asking more questions than Mrs Paterson and the police put together. Her mother could play the dottery old fool when it suited her, but she was obviously still as sharp as a tack.

'Don't be silly – I never hated her,' Kat said.

'You're talking like she's deed. You do think something's happened to her, don't you?' Maureen was enjoying herself.

'No, I – I mean… I don't know but when someone goes missing and they're not found after a while you begin to fear the worst.'

'Spit it out, Katherine – tell me what you know.'

'I don't know anything, honestly.'

'You're glad she's gone missing though, aren't you?'

'No, of course not.'

'I could always tell when you were lying; you were never any good at it. I caught you out every single time when you were younger. You've no' exactly got a good poker face.' Maureen laughed.

'I'm not lying, Mum. Okay, I didn't like her, but I don't know anything about what's happened to her.'

If Kat was crumbling in a conversation with her elderly mother, what would she be like if the police did eventually catch up with her again? She'd be bang to rights.

'Why didn't you like her?' Maureen wasn't for letting it go. She was like a dog with a bone.

'Will you just leave it, Mum? The girl's missing; hopefully she'll be found soon,' Kat said, trying to shut the conversation down.

'Still doesn't change the fact you hated the poor wee lassie.'

'Poor wee lassie? What kind of poor wee lassie terrorizes someone for absolutely no reason? What kind of poor wee lassie comes round, gains access to your house and kills your fucking cat!' Kat had lost her temper and she instantly regretted it.

'What? She killed Kiddles? She terrorized you?' Maureen said, stunned at her daughter's outburst.

Kat was in tears now; there was a mixture of anger and relief spilling out of her. It felt good to eventually tell someone about the bullying. She hadn't told a single soul apart from Tony in the months it had been going on.

'Yeah, she killed my cat and she's been bullying me in work for months now,' Kat said through the tears.

'How could you let this go on? You need to—'

'Mum, I really don't need a lecture, and I don't want you telling anyone else anything about it. I want you to promise me you won't repeat a word of what I just said.'

'What?

'Mum.'

'Who do you think I'm going to tell? Half of the folk in here can't remember how to tie their shoelaces…'

'Promise me, Mum.'

'Katherine, I promise. I'll not say a word about it. I'll tell you one thing though… I hope the little cow has come to a sticky end.'

49

Archie Thomson was pushing seventy years old but was still responsible – either directly or indirectly – for a large portion of all organised crime taking place in Glasgow. Drugs, prostitution, robberies, human trafficking – you name it, Archie Thomson had his grubby paws all over it. However, he was a slippery customer. He always had a ready alibi or some stooge to take the fall. He also never personally touched anything illegal. He hadn't served a sentence in a Scottish prison since a two-year stint in Barlinnie around twenty years ago.

Prentice and Donaldson knew Thomson spent a lot of his time in an office next to one of his many nail bars – who knew gangsters like him knew so much about women's nails? Prentice opened the door of the office without knocking. Their luck was in – Archie was in residence.

'Officers, to what do I owe the pleasure of your visit today?' Thomson said, a large smile engulfing his weasel face.

'Morning, Archie. We were wondering if we could have a word about Rachel Strang?' Prentice said before Donaldson got the chance to talk.

'Rachel Strang? You'll need to help me out here, boys.'

'She's engaged to your nephew – Jason,' Donaldson said as he took in the surroundings.

'Jason? I didn't even know he was seeing a lassie, never mind engaged. Truth be told, I thought the boy was gay.' Archie laughed. 'Anyway, I'm a busy man so let's get this moving… what's happened to the lassie?'

'Miss Strang has disappeared. We were wondering if you had any idea of her whereabouts?' Prentice said. Both detectives knew this meeting would get them absolutely nowhere, but they had to meet him. Archie Thomson wouldn't help them even if he could.

'She's probably ran away before she has to marry that big numpty Lurch.' Thomson laughed at his own joke. 'Honestly, boys, you've had a wasted journey. I couldn't tell you the first thing about this wee girl. I'll need to get in touch with Jason though, congratulate the big lanky streak of piss for finally finding someone daft enough to marry him!'

Donaldson was already turning to leave. He hated Archie Thomson more than he hated most of the Glasgow criminal fraternity. Thomson found great pleasure in giving Police Scotland the runaround. He would always make time for them, knowing full well that they had nothing they could put him away for.

'Do you think Jason could be involved in anything that might endanger his fiancée?' Prentice asked.

'Jason? I doubt it very much. Although saying that – he's not the brightest is our Jason, so who's to say?' Thomson said.

'Archie, if you do find out anything or if Jason is involved in something that's led to Rachel getting into bother then give me a call.' Prentice handed his card to the old gangster, who pocketed it. Everyone in the room knew there would be no phone calls forthcoming.

'Aye, no bother, chaps.' Archie smiled. 'I'll be on the bell with any information I come across.'

'Thanks for your time, Archie,' Prentice said, heading for the door. Donaldson was already halfway out it.

'Is that it? No' much of an interrogation that. You need to brush up on your interviewing skills, lads,' Thomson said. 'Sure you don't want to pop in next door and get your nails done?' He was enjoying himself.

'See you soon, Mr Thomson,' Prentice said.

'I'll look forward to it.'

50

Kat hadn't meant to tell anyone about the bullying and the abuse she had been subjected to. She had just blurted it out after her mother referred to Rachel as a 'poor wee lassie'. She couldn't help herself. Hearing Rachel referred to like that had pressed all of the wrong buttons. Couple that with constantly having to see the 'butter wouldn't melt' photo of her that every newspaper and online site was forcing down their throats. Kat's outburst served as a timely warning that she could easily blow the whole thing. Her mother had promised Kat that she wouldn't tell a living soul and Kat had believed her. That wasn't the point though, was it? She still shouldn't have said it. What would happen if the police asked some questions she didn't like? She needed to get a grip of herself.

Kat had decided the next step to take. She had thought it through and determined it needed her full concentration, so she had thought about nothing else for the entirety of her shift. Every single person caught up in this sorry mess should be told exactly what had been going on. The part about Kat being involved would conveniently be omitted. Kat couldn't just sit back and leave everything to chance. She had to try to make sure the finger of blame would never point her way. Kat had reasoned that if everyone was suspecting Stephen or Kirsty (or even Tony and Jason) for the disappearance and subsequent murder of Rachel then they wouldn't be considering Kat.

She had bought a cheap pay-as-you-go phone from another busy newsagent in the city centre on the way home from work on Friday. She knew the police would have great trouble trying to trace any messages sent from it and she would be ditching the phone as soon as it had served its purpose. In the unlikely event that the texts could somehow be traced – and Kat was sure that they couldn't be – she had decided to send them from a busy location. She wasn't going to send them from her flat in any case. So she took a seat on Saturday morning at one of the benches on George Square, facing away from the cameras looking down from above. There were people all around and she was sure no one would notice her sending the messages and reading the numbers from her notepad.

Kat had a list of all the numbers she would need, a list that she would be tearing to shreds as soon as the messages were sent. She was going to gather everyone together for what was sure to be an explosive meeting.

Kat had thought long and hard about her plan, and her mind was made up. The one thing she was sure of was that she wanted to be there when it all happened. She wanted to see it. Obviously, she couldn't be physically at the meeting but she wanted it to happen in a place where she could have a good vantage point. A place of her choosing. She had plumped for somewhere which was clearly visible from her mum's flat, which she still hadn't put up for sale yet. It overlooked the far end of Kelvingrove Park and had great views. This meant that if she scheduled the meet for the south entrance to the park then she would be able to clearly see what happened.

Kat had bought the phone to help speed things along. She composed her first text, which was to Jason. She sent details of the meet along with some interesting information. He would definitely be in attendance, Kat was sure of it.

> Stepdad Ste has been having an affair with Rachel. He knows where she is. Meet at the south entrance to Kelvingrove Park on Lydon St at 3 p.m. today. More will be revealed.

Kat tried to spell it out as clearly as she could to Jason, as judging by his texts and voicemails he wasn't going to be a contestant on *Mastermind* anytime soon. The text would set the cat amongst the pigeons, she was sure of that. Jason would struggle to hold his temper. Kat had set the meeting for that afternoon to avoid everyone meeting up beforehand – she was sure there was no way Jason wouldn't have gone looking for Stephen.

Right away, the phone started ringing and it was Jason's number. Kat stared at the handset; there was no way she was going to answer.

A text came through less than a minute later.

Who the fuck's this?

What a charmer he was. Kat wasn't going to reply to the text. She composed her next message. It was to Tony.

Finally ready to meet. Sorry for messing you about. Trouble with Jason and my stepdad. Was a bit scary for a bit. All will be explained. Meet me at…

Kirsty was next.

Sorry for disappearing. Everything got a bit much for me plus Tony has been hassling me. He wants us to be more than friends. Meet me at…

The phone was ringing again. This time it was Kirsty. Again, Kat wasn't going to answer. She waited for the call to end and sent the next message. To Rachel's mum, Laura.

For more information about your daughter's disappearance meet at…

Kat couldn't bring herself to pretend the message was from Rachel – she didn't want to give her even more false hope that her daughter was still alive and well. She wasn't that callous or heartless. The star of this particular show would receive the next text. Stephen. Kat felt a great deal of power having his number in her possession and his life in her hands. She had to make sure he turned up to the meeting.

Rachel and her manager Tony have been having an affair. He
knows where she is. Meet at…

The final text was the most vital if her plan was going to work. Kat had
wondered how she could get the police to attend the meeting without actually
calling them. She really didn't want that to happen as they would have a
recording of the call and it would be investigated thoroughly. She had found
an anonymous text line for Crimestoppers online. She hoped the message
would be taken seriously.

All suspects in the disappearance of Rachel Strang will be at…

Then she took out the sim card, tried her best to snap it and dropped it to
the ground. She scraped it with her foot into a drain. She would dispose of
the phone when she went out later.

Kat smiled. She left her seat and walked in the direction of the subway
station at Buchanan Street. She would go to her mother's flat soon and
prepare to watch the meeting.

Everything had been set in motion. Her work here was done.

51

Prentice and his team had spent hours at the bank and hadn't gained much insight into Rachel Strang's character or her current whereabouts. Many of the team, including his partner Donaldson, were of the opinion that it had been a complete waste of time, but Prentice knew that any information gleaned about Rachel Strang would be beneficial to the enquiry and they couldn't afford not to interview her workmates. Donaldson was also still fuming at being dragged to meet Archie Thomson. He had told Prentice that no good would come from it but Prentice had insisted.

Prentice wasn't one to cut corners. He knew many of his colleagues made fun of him and his methods behind his back, but he didn't care. He didn't do the job to make friends. He was never going to win over many of his fellow detectives because he wasn't 'one of them'. He hadn't worked his way through uniform for years and toiled like the majority of them. He had been fast-tracked through a graduate programme from university and many used it as a stick to beat him with. It didn't matter to them that, more often than not, he got results. Maybe it irked them that he got better results than they did. Whatever it was, there was nothing Prentice could do to change their opinion of him so he had stopped even trying.

Prentice and the team had been at the Strang house again as well today. Forensics had been with them and they would search the whole place from top to bottom. If something had happened to Rachel in that house or its surrounding gardens then it would be uncovered. They had already taken away the family car for a forensic examination, and they were currently going over the house and garden with a fine-tooth comb. It was vital that nothing was missed. Prentice couldn't afford any cock-ups. Not with the top brass and the press watching their every move.

Word had come through to Prentice and Donaldson that there had been an interesting development in the case. A piece of information had come via Crimestoppers and it was being taken very seriously. If what was being claimed was true then it could go a long way to solving the case.

The tip-off had come through by text mid-morning Saturday. Donaldson wasn't even sure how that was possible, but they were both pleased that it had.

The text talked about a meeting between all parties involved in the disappearance of Rachel. Prentice and Donaldson didn't know what to expect, but they weren't going to ignore the information. The police hadn't had long to set up an operation but set up one they had – both Prentice and Donaldson sat in an unmarked car across from the entrance to Kelvingrove Park eager to see what would happen. There were officers sprinkled everywhere around the park, both plain clothes and uniform. The helicopter would also come into play if it all went pear-shaped. Prentice loved this bit of the job. The adrenaline flowing in his veins. The anticipation that something was about to happen. Something that could have a huge bearing on whether they found Rachel Strang dead or alive.

52

Kat was all set up in her mother's flat. She had moved one of the dining-room chairs over to the window which would give her a near perfect view of what was going to unfold. She had sent the texts only a few hours previously, but she was sure that every recipient would show at the park.

Kat didn't like to admit it to herself but she was excited. Today was the day. She couldn't wait until the whole thing blew up. If truth be told, she would be glad when the whole thing was at an end and she could resume living her life again without fear of being caught. It really was stressing her out no end. If Kat could make it look like Stephen (and hopefully Kirsty) had something to do with Rachel's disappearance then the police would never even look into her.

Kat was perfectly positioned to watch the upcoming event. She knew she shouldn't be within one hundred miles of the park, but she couldn't help it – she needed to see what happened. This must be what Mrs Paterson felt like. Kat had reasoned that there was no way the police would be looking for her, especially with all that was going to happen. She could see police officers stationed at different parts of the park, and she was sure some of the cars parked around the place were filled with officers out of uniform. She hoped that was the case. It looked like they were taking her text seriously.

Kat had made sure the blinds were drawn, but she had left enough of a gap to see everything that happened across the road at the park's entrance. Kat was certain that no one would be looking up at the window, but she was still cautious. Kat could see everything. The unobstructed view was spectacular. Although, annoyingly, she wouldn't be able to hear what would be said. There was nothing that could be done about that, but she reasoned she could probably guess the dialogue anyway. Everything was set. Let the games begin...

After what seemed like an eternity, the main players started to arrive. Stephen was the first on the scene and he looked shifty as hell. He hopped from one leg to the next and fidgeted. He hadn't heard from Rachel – as far as he knew his sordid little secret was still safe. All he knew was that he had received a text saying to be there as it regarded Rachel's whereabouts. The text had said her manager in work knew more about it and he was having an affair with her. After what they had been up to, Stephen wasn't too surprised. He was hoping beyond hope that Rachel would show up, alive and well. He had never been so worried about someone before. He hadn't even been sleeping.

Tony arrived next. The two men looked each other over. They had never met before, but it seemed clear that they were both waiting on someone.

'Are you Tony?' Stephen asked. He had taken a leap of faith by confronting the man standing beside him in the park. He couldn't put his finger on it, but somehow he knew the man was here because of Rachel.

'Yeah, how'd you know that? Where's Rachel? Is she here? Who are you?' Tony said. He was clearly agitated.

'I got told you knew where she was. I got a message saying you've been having an affair with Rachel! What have you done with her? Where is she?' Stephen said, trying to restrain himself from grabbing Tony by the neck.

'An affair? What you talking about? I've no idea where Rach—' Tony began talking but was quickly interrupted.

It was when Jason arrived that the real fun and games began. Kat thought this might happen after reading all about Jason's anger issues.

Jason was an 'actions speak louder than words' type of guy – he ran quickly and directly for Stephen. He threw a punch at Stephen's face and it connected. His fist burst Stephen's nose, sending blood spurting everywhere. Kat shuddered from the window – even she could feel the impact of the punch. It rocketed Stephen's head backwards, but somehow he managed to keep his feet.

'What you doing? Get off me!' Stephen shouted whilst trying to hold his nose together. Tony tried to hold Jason back. It was turning into *The Jeremy Kyle Show* already. Tony was elbowed in the side of the head in the struggle.

'You're her stepdad for fuck's sake!' Jason shouted whilst still trying to land punches.

'What's he talking about?' The very special guest had arrived, just in the nick of time – Rachel's mum, Laura. Why should she miss out on all the fun? Jason stepped back.

'Your lovely husband here has been shagging your daughter. My fiancée! Has been for months!' Jason said, clenching his fists, ready for another chance to inflict pain on Stephen.

Stephen, nose bloodied, looked as if he was about to run away or burst into tears. He wanted the ground to swallow him up. He hadn't known what to expect after getting the text message, but he wasn't expecting or prepared for an ambush like this.

'I've not touched Rachel – honestly, Laura!' Stephen didn't sound convincing. He had tears welling up in his eyes, and blood was pouring from his nose as he spluttered out his feeble defence.

Laura didn't look like a woman to be trifled with. After only a moment's hesitation, she had made up her mind.

'I knew something was going on with you. I knew it, but I never imagined this.' Laura shook her head, thinking it over. 'You and Rachel! I'll rip your fuckin balls off!' she screamed.

She stormed towards Stephen, swinging and connecting with punches and kicks.

'I've not done anything!' Stephen said as he tried to protect his head from the blows.

Tony had taken a few punches himself but again he had managed to split it all up. He didn't think when he'd been invited to the park it was to be a bouncer.

'Who the hell are you?' Laura shouted as Tony dragged her off. 'Get your hands off me.'

'He's Tony, Rachel's manager at work,' Stephen spluttered through all the blood, snot and tears. 'He's the one who's been having an affair with Rachel – not me!'

All eyes turned to Tony. Jason looked especially keen to hear what his reply would be.

'What? He's trying to save his own skin! I'm just her manager. He's the one been having the affair!' Tony said, pointing at the mess that was Stephen. This seemed enough explanation for Jason and Laura – they both lunged for Stephen again.

Kirsty arrived to a scene of absolute carnage.

'Dad! What the hell's going on here?' she screamed. A sizeable crowd was now gathering to watch. Many of them had their mobile phones out, recording the melee.

Jason and Laura temporarily halted their assault.

'Your dad, my beloved husband here, has been having an affair with Rachel! My own flesh and blood!' Laura Strang shouted.

'What? No way. No chance. Dad?' Kirsty asked.

'It's nonsense, love; I'd never touch Rachel. Not like that…'

'Where is she?' Kirsty said.

'I don't know. Honestly, love, I've not done anything. I got a message saying Tony here knows where she is – message said they'd been having an affair at work,' Stephen said.

Everyone stopped and turned their attention to Tony again.

'Is this right?' Kirsty said. 'I knew you two had been acting funny at work.'

This was more than enough for Jason; he lunged at Tony this time. Tony had seen what had happened to Stephen – he wasn't hanging around for the same treatment. He started to run; Jason followed. It looked like an episode of *The Benny Hill Show* with the two of them running around in circles. Some of the crowd laughed as they filmed the ridiculous scene on their phones.

'Does anyone know where my daughter is?' Laura screamed at the top of her voice and everyone stopped.

They all stood for a moment, looking around at each other. This was the real reason they had been called together. Someone here knew more than they were letting on.

'Somebody better start talking because I've had just about enough of this!' Laura said.

The police had also had enough. They had watched and listened to the mayhem unfold and now appeared from every direction. There were loads of them.

Kat couldn't take her eyes from the scene unfolding in front of her eyes. The messages had worked even better than she had anticipated. This was all happening because of her. She was the orchestrator now.

The police tried unsuccessfully to calm the situation down. Jason was bundled to the ground by four or five officers – they put handcuffs on him as he struggled on the ground. The police would definitely call it resisting arrest. Laura stood screaming at everyone and anyone who would listen, whilst Kirsty tried to tend to Stephen and his injuries. Tony stood still – he looked shocked at the whole situation. The sizeable crowd continued filming with their mobile phones. The whole carry-on would be posted on social media imminently no doubt. Kat kept watching from the window. It was absolute carnage. She found to her surprise that she was smiling.

Stephen, Jason, Tony, Kirsty and Laura were all led to waiting police vans. It looked like they were all being detained and taken in for questioning. The interviews would be very interesting, to say the least. Kat was now as sure as she could be that her name wouldn't enter calculations with all of these potential suspects. Why would any suspicion fall upon her?

53

Kat was absolutely exhausted by the time she got home. She hadn't been sleeping properly and it had been a long, eventful day. She needed some food and a rest on the couch. However, just as she was taking off her jacket, the buzzer went. Whoever it was could wait. Kat didn't want to see anyone.

She looked through the peephole. Surprise, surprise – it was Mrs Paterson. Not what she needed. Although her elderly neighbour was holding a plate stacked high with food. At least that was something. Kat's stomach was growling she was that hungry. She opened the door.

'Mrs Paterson, you'll really need to stop cooking for me,' Kat said, taking the proffered plate. 'I really appreciate it though – it smells lovely.'

Mrs Paterson had a concerned look on her face. It was the same face she'd made when Kiddles had died.

'What's wrong? Are you okay?'

'I'm fine. It's just… well, I'll come right out and say it. The girl.'

'What girl?' Kat said.

'The girl from your work. The one who's on the news.'

'What about her?' Kat wasn't expecting this; it was a worrying turn of events.

'It's just. I saw her, didn't I? The other day, she was coming out of here. Wasn't she?'

'Rachel Strang?' Kat didn't know what to say. She should have been prepared for Mrs Paterson seeing her – she saw just about everything else.

'Yes, Rachel Strang. The girl who's gone missing,' Mrs Paterson said with a hint of irritation in her voice now.

'Yeah. She was here. She was just dropping off some work stuff for me. Terrible business her going missing like that. Everyone's just praying she's found safe and well.'

'I knew it was her,' Mrs Paterson said. She looked pleased with herself now. 'The thing is though, do I phone the number that's on the news bulletins? Do I let the police know that I've seen her?'

'Oh, don't worry about that,' Kat said, trying to keep the concern from her voice. 'The police have already spoken to me. I've told them all about it. It wasn't actually the last time we saw one another. I saw her in the office after that. So the police weren't really interested that she'd come here. I felt like I was wasting their time, to be honest.' Kat was glad she had opened the door and let Mrs Paterson in. She hoped her explanation would be enough to dissuade her neighbour from dialling the number.

'That's a weight off my mind, Kat, I can tell you. I was just about to phone them and then I thought I'd better run it past you first. I'm so glad I did. I've been worrying about this since I saw her picture.'

Of all the things Kat had listed that might lead to her arrest, her elderly neighbour hadn't crossed her mind. She should have known Mrs Paterson would have clocked Rachel. She hadn't foreseen her elderly neighbour bringing the police to her door and possibly bringing the whole case crumbling down upon her.

'No need to worry. Hopefully she'll be found soon,' Kat said.

'I hope so, but the longer this goes on, it's not looking good, is it?' Mrs Paterson said.

'No, I'm afraid it's not.' It's not looking good for Rachel at all, she thought.

54

The tip-off had proved to be spot on. Everyone involved in the rammy at the park had been taken in for interrogation. The only question that remained for Prentice was who had sent the text message to let them know what was happening in the first place? No one else seemed to be concerned about it, least of all Donaldson. They were just pleased that someone had had the foresight to inform them.

The interviews were time-consuming but very informative. There was a wide range of emotions on show. Rachel's mother, Laura Strang, was first up. She had been in an angry rage all the way to the station and took a good while to calm down enough so the interview could actually take place. She was furious, and both Prentice and Donaldson couldn't blame her one little bit.

'Will the two of you explain to me what the hell is going on here?' Laura said as soon as the detectives entered the small interview room.

'We realise you're upset, Laura, but we want the same thing you do. We want Rachel found,' Prentice said.

This seemed to focus her for a moment. 'Aye, we want her found. Of course we do,' she said, 'but it's like everyone knows something I don't?'

Donaldson started first: 'Did you suspect your husband might have been—'

'Shagging my daughter? Are you for real? If I'd suspected that do you honestly think I'd have kept the dirty fucker in my house... in my bed?' Laura said. 'So no, Mr Donaldson. I didn't suspect Ste would do anything like that, and I hope you people are looking into him because I'll tell you this, that lying, two-faced little weasel knows more than he's letting on. He either knows where Rachel is or he's ki—' Laura broke off. Everyone knew what she couldn't bring herself to say.

'Would you like a break, Laura?' Prentice asked.

'No,' Laura said. 'I just want this over; I just want my daughter back.'

'We know that. We're doing everything we can,' Prentice said.

'Do you think she's dead?' Laura asked, tears forming in her eyes.

'I'll be straight with you. No one can say for certain either way, but the longer it goes with no contact then… it's looking less likely Rachel's came to no harm. We're looking into every aspect of her life, and I know it doesn't seem like it, but we're making progress,' Prentice said. He'd jumped in with the answer as he was sure Donaldson would have been a hell of a lot blunter in his response.

'Do you see much of Archie Thomson?' Donaldson asked.

'Jason's uncle? No. Jason claims he's close to him, but I thought it was a lot of rubbish. He really is his uncle then?' Laura asked.

'Yeah, he's his uncle. So he doesn't come around the house then?' Prentice said.

'Nope. I've never even met him. Jason likes to use his name, make himself look like the big man, but he tells a lot of tall tales does that boy,' Laura said.

'We'd like to ask you about Stephen – or Ste as he seems to be known. We know you had no idea he was involved with Rachel, but you said at the park that you knew he was up to something. Can you tell us what you meant?' Donaldson said. He wanted to get out of the interview as quickly as possible so he was trying to speed things along.

'Ste's always up to something. He's always bloody lying or got some madcap scheme on the go to try and make a quick buck and now this? Well, this is the final straw. I'm done with him. You need to look at Ste though. I think he knows where Rachel is or he's done something to her—'

'Has Ste ever been violent with you?' Prentice asked.

'Violent? No chance. I'd batter him, but Rachel's not like me – she's not as streetwise. She's too soft. So would he be violent with her? Is that what you're thinking? I don't know. I'd have said there was no chance of that either, but then I didn't even spot the two of them together so what the hell do I know?'

She had no idea where Rachel was or if she was even still alive. All she knew was that her husband had been having an affair with her own daughter. Her life had completely crumbled. Both officers were sure she had nothing to do with Rachel's disappearance.

'Who organised the meeting at the park?' Prentice said. His curiosity got the better of him.

'I don't know,' Laura said. 'I got a text message telling me to go there and more information would be revealed or something like that. I didn't know everyone would be there.'

Prentice had thought that might be the case. It annoyed him that no one knew who had organised the meeting.

'In the circumstances, I think we'd be better concluding this interview just now and trying to find out from a few of the others that were at the park what's happened to Rachel. You've got my number though, so phone me if anything happens or you think of anything else,' Prentice said. Donaldson was already ushering Laura out of the room.

55

Rachel's boss from the bank was a snivelling mess. Tony McPherson was in floods of tears before Prentice and Donaldson had even begun to ask a question.

'Tony, what you bubbling for? You're not responsible for the disappearance of Rachel, are you?' Donaldson asked.

Tony's lawyer handed his client a tissue, which Tony loudly used, much to the consternation of the two detectives. They both winced as he blew his nose before speaking. 'No. No, I just want her back so bad.'

'Why do you want her back so bad? She can't be that good an employee?' Prentice said before Donaldson could say something similar but ruder.

'You don't understand. I love her. She's everything to me.' Tony sniffed.

'You can't be everything to her though, can you?' Donaldson again. 'She's getting married soon and she's been getting slipped a length from her stepdaddy.' Donaldson looked like he was enjoying himself. Prentice gave him a stern look which he tried to ignore.

'She was going to leave Jason; she just hadn't built up the courage to tell him it was over. There was no way she would marry a Neanderthal like that,' Tony said, dabbing his eyes with his tissue.

'What about Stephen Armstrong? The "stepdaddy" as my colleague puts it?' Prentice said.

'I don't believe a word of it. There's no way she'd cheat on me like that. No way and that's the end of it.'

'No, Tony boy, that's far from the end of it. You and I both know that

Rachel likes to put it about.'

Donaldson was going to go into one; Prentice had seen this before. He knew the mess sitting across from him wasn't ready to hear it, but there was no putting it off. He needed a reality check more than most so he let his colleague continue.

'She's got, by my count, three blokes on the go and who's to say that's where it ends? Maybe she's got a whole football team lined up. You, Tony my friend, are the runt of the litter. She's been using you more than most. Now, let's get down to the nitty gritty. Stop fucking about and tell us. Do you know what's happened to her? Do you know if she's still alive?'

The thought that Rachel was dead seemed to be a new idea to Tony. A new thought he wasn't prepared for. He started wailing again. The tears were in full flow. Even the lawyer looked to the heavens in exasperation.

Donaldson and Prentice looked at each other. Without saying a word, they both knew they were thinking the same thing: Tony McPherson didn't have it in him. He was besotted with Rachel, but he was not the man they were after.

56

There was nothing more Kat could do. She polished off the meal Mrs Paterson had prepared for her and lay back on the couch with her feet up. She could barely move off her chair – a combination of the tiredness at not sleeping properly since Rachel's demise and the massive amount of home-made casserole she had just demolished. It was the first proper meal she'd eaten since the fateful incident.

The day's events spun in her head. She wondered about everyone who had been taken away in the police vans, and she smiled at the thought that she was responsible for it all happening. If it wasn't for her then the police wouldn't be any further forward in their enquiries. They'd still be scratching around like headless chickens looking for Rachel. Kat was glad Mrs Paterson had knocked on her door, and not only for providing the lovely home-cooked meal that had gone down a treat. The old lady could easily have put her foot in it by telling the police that she had seen Rachel visiting Kat. It would have led to many awkward questions, not least why Kat hadn't bothered to inform the police about it. Hopefully, Mrs Paterson would take Kat at her word and not phone the information in.

There was nothing else Kat could do just now in any case. She had done her level best to try to point the finger of guilt at Stephen, but if the police didn't go for it then there wasn't much she could do about that. For the first time since this all began she felt a little helpless. Things were now being taken out of her hands. She would have to rely on the police not classing her as a person of interest.

Kat wondered how the police interviews were going. She wondered what they would all say to the police. How would they react? Who would the police be looking at as suspects? Kat turned it all over and over again in her head.

Kat was sure of one thing though. She was absolutely exhausted. She was doing herself no favours at all by avoiding sleep and proper eating. If the tiredness persisted she was bound to make a vital mistake which could cost her everything, including her freedom. Kat set the alarm on her phone for the morning, closed her eyes and lay back on the couch. She tried to stop worrying about things out with her control and let herself drift off. Within two minutes she was fast asleep.

57

The fiancé Jason Thomson was a more interesting candidate. An altogether better fit. Prentice liked the boyfriend as a suspect. His uncle would have the means to dispose of a body, no question about it. He'd done it many times before and still hadn't been caught. Prentice and many others had tried for years to make something stick to him, but he always wriggled out of it. Archie Thomson was the Teflon man, and it had led to many of the Glasgow underworld coming to the conclusion that he was a grass.

The only sticking point to Jason as a good fit for the murder – and make no mistake about it, the vast majority of the detectives on the case were convinced this was murder – was the fact he actually name-dropped his uncle. He wanted to be known as some sort of gangster it seemed, but when the question of his guilt was asked outright he shrivelled up beneath their eyes. He was like a little boy who was one step away from asking if his mother could sit in with him instead of the duty solicitor. No, Prentice wasn't convinced about Jason's murder-suspect credentials. Donaldson wasn't having any of it.

'Why do you feel the need to tell us your uncle is some two-bit gangster?' Donaldson was in no mood for niceties. He hated name-droppers with a passion. He used to work with a guy who constantly told anyone unfortunate enough to be listening that he had once played football in the same team as George Best. It was a complete and utter lie.

'Whit? My uncle's no two-bit gangster. He's feared, mate,' Jason said. He put his hands behind his mop of blonde hair and looked like he wanted to put his feet up. The solicitor looked to the ceiling; he'd seen this all before.

'Feared? Don't make me laugh, son,' Donaldson replied. 'Why don't you take that stupid grin off your face and help us find out what's happened to your lovely little fiancée, eh? The way we hear it, she's been putting it about left, right and centre.'

Jason's grin swiftly disappeared. 'Don't you dare speak about her like that.' He was standing now and looked like he wanted to pick a fight. 'Don't you fuc—'

'Sit down. Tell us about Rachel. Where do you think she is?' Prentice had seen enough. Jason had been riled by Donaldson's comments, but he wasn't sure how far it would get them with their enquiries.

Jason did as he was told. Sat down. 'I don't know where she is. I've tried phoning her, texting her, looking for her everywhere. I've even phoned a couple of her pals. She's nowhere. I can't find her.'

'Do you think she's come to harm?' Prentice asked.

'I dunno. Probably. It's not looking like she's coming home anyway.'

'Do you think she could have done a runner? Maybe there's someone else on the scene we don't know about and she's away with them?' Donaldson said. 'I mean she's engaged to you, seeing her boss at work and having it away with her bloody stepdad. Who's to say there's not any more? Maybe it all got a bit too much for her?'

Jason scowled at Donaldson. 'Listen, that bastard Ste is the one you should be speaking to. He's the one. I'm telling ye. He knows what's happened to Rachel. I'm sure of it.'

'What makes you so sure?' Prentice asked.

'He's a fucking liar, that's what makes me sure. He's always had some sort of hold over Rachel and her stepsister. They both worship the ground he walks on for some reason. He snaps his fingers and they both jump.'

'Who's to say that you've not done anything to Rachel?' Donaldson said. 'You seem to have a temper – maybe you found out she was having an affair with her stepdad and you snapped? Did something you regret?'

'No chance. You're not pinning this on me.'

'Maybe your best buddy Uncle Archie helped you get rid of the body?' Donaldson said.

'Uncle Archie had nothing to do with any of this. He's... he's never even met Rachel.'

'So you did this all yourself then?' Donaldson continued.

'I'd never do anything to hurt Rachel,' Jason said. 'I... I love her.' And with that he burst into tears. The transformation from wannabe gangster to a teary-eyed teenager was quick and complete. Maybe he wasn't such a good fit for the disappearance after all, Prentice thought.

'People do strange things in the name of love,' Donaldson said.

'No,' Jason said through tears, which were streaming down his face now. 'I just want her back; I need her. Please find her. Please.'

58

There was definitely something fishy about Stephen Armstrong's daughter Kirsty. She had no reason to be that obstructive. She had no reason to be that defensive. She didn't seem to want to help progress the enquiry in any way, shape or form, or realise the seriousness of the situation.

'You know your dad's bang to rights here, and I think you've got something to do with all of this.' Donaldson started the interview with a bang.

'No,' Kirsty said.

'Is that all you've got to say?' Prentice asked. 'Your father has been having an affair with your stepsister, who is missing – who could be dead for all you know – and all you can say is "No"?'

'I've got nothing to do with any of this,' Kirsty said, folding her arms in some sort of attempt at looking confident. It didn't work.

'You know your dad's in this up to his neck though?' Donaldson asked.

'I don't believe that either. There's no way Dad would risk—' Kirsty stopped herself from speaking.

'Risk what?' Prentice said.

'Nothing. It's nothing.'

'What wouldn't your dad risk, Kirsty?' Prentice asked again.

'I don't know what you're talking about.'

'What do you think about your dad sleeping with Rachel?' Donaldson said, trying a different line of attack.

'No chance,' Kirsty replied.

'No chance? So everyone's lying?' Donaldson didn't like this girl one bit.

Her attitude was stinking.

'Ask them,' Kirsty said, looking at the floor.

'Listen to me,' Prentice said. He too was getting annoyed by this girl's reluctance to help them. 'Your stepsister is missing. Could be dead or in grave danger, and you're sitting there pissing us about. If you know anything then you need to let us know, and you need to let us know now.'

'I don't know anything. I don't. Honestly,' Kirsty said, unable to meet either detective's eye. Prentice and Donaldson looked far from convinced.

'How did you feel when you and your dad moved in with Rachel and her mother?' Prentice asked, trying yet another different approach.

'What's that got to do with anything?' Kirsty said.

'I take it you weren't best pleased then?' Prentice said.

'No, not at first, but after a while it was alright,' Kirsty said. 'We got along quite well, me and Rachel.'

'So there's no reason whatsoever that you would like to see her come to harm?' Donaldson said.

'No. None.'

'Is there anywhere you can think of that Rachel might have gone?' Prentice asked.

'No.' Kirsty shook her head. She was annoying both detectives with how obstructive she was being. If she got along well with Rachel as she claimed, she would be more concerned than this.

'Is there anyone who would like to see Rachel come to harm? Anyone with a grudge against her?' Donaldson said.

'Not that I can think of,' Kirsty said, crossing her arms again. It was infuriating.

'Listen here.' Donaldson was on the verge of really losing his temper. He couldn't believe the young girl's attitude. 'Your stepsister is in serious danger – that is if she's not come to grief already. Now, you need to have a good look at yourself and start helping. Not telling us anything ain't going to do you any favours, and it's certainly not going to help Rachel. Tell us what you know or I'm going to—'

'What my colleague is saying is that it might not be too late to help

Rachel,' Prentice interrupted. 'Tell us anything that can help us bring her home safely.'

'I don't know how many different ways I can tell you both. I don't know anything,' Kirsty said.

If Kirsty had anything whatsoever to do with the disappearance of Rachel then both Prentice and Donaldson would enjoy making sure she faced serious charges.

59

Stephen Armstrong was the last of those detained at the park to be interviewed. He had to be patched up first by a doctor. Remarkably his nose wasn't broken. He'd have bad bruising around his nose and eyes, but apart from that the doctor was happy for him to be questioned.

The formalities out of the way, the interview began.

'Stephen, do you know where Rachel Strang is?' Prentice asked. Stephen looked as nervous a man as both detectives had ever witnessed. He was fidgeting. He was sweating profusely.

'No,' he replied, looking pleadingly at his lawyer as if the duty solicitor could magically make all of this go away.

'If you're not involved in this, and I can't see that for one second, then you know who is,' Prentice said. 'Where is Rachel?'

'I don't know,' Stephen said. 'Honestly, I've got no idea where she is.' Honesty and Stephen Armstrong didn't make good bedfellows.

'You've been having an inappropriate relationship with her, haven't you?' Prentice said.

'What? That's nonsense.'

'Nonsense?' Donaldson said. 'So why did the big fella smash you in the face then?'

'It's... it's a misunderstanding. That's all.' Stephen was far from convincing.

'Aye, that's all it is,' Donaldson said, voice rising. 'A wee misunderstanding. Nothing to see here. Move along. What a load of utter bollocks! Do us, and yourself, a favour and cooperate with us. Don't sit there and spin us a pack of lies. There's a good chance the poor girl is in danger. Now tell us what you know.'

Stephen's lawyer remained impassive even with his client's pleading looks. Stephen was going to have to make up his own mind whether to tell the truth or not.

'Okay, Rachel liked me a little too much and she tried to—'

'Is that what you're going to come away with?' Donaldson interrupted. 'Is that what you expect us to believe? Rachel fancied you, you told her, "No chance, I'm in a loving relationship with your maw," and she's run off? Is that the nonsense you're going to spout?' Donaldson was convinced of Stephen's guilt already.

Stephen looked terrified. 'Eh… no, it's just… I don't know what you want me to say.'

'Stephen, we want the truth. That's all,' Prentice said.

Stephen sat in silence and nervously rubbed at his chin, wondering what he should say or how he could wheedle his way out of this. He came up short.

'Right, let's try something else,' Prentice said. 'We've spoken to you a few times now, Stephen, about your stepdaughter's disappearance. What do you think's happened to her?'

'I don't know. Honestly. I've no idea,' Stephen said. He sounded like his daughter. Neither he or Kirsty were coming across well. It was like the two of them didn't want to help find Rachel.

The detectives weren't going to get much more out of him. Without any concrete evidence, he was just going to stick to his lies. Prentice and Donaldson knew they needed more. Prentice reluctantly brought the interview to a close; Donaldson stormed out of the room before he punched a wall – or worse, the suspect. However, within less than a minute he was back outside the door, a smile wide on his face.

'Shannon from forensics has just told me,' Donaldson said. He couldn't help grinning. Prentice waited eagerly for him to continue. 'They've found spots of blood in the shed and on the couch in the shed. Plus, they've found her phone. It's him. We've got him.'

60

I can't believe it looks like Rachel set me up. I know we were only stepsisters but it felt like real sisters to me.

Who am I kidding?

I'll sort her out when she comes back. She can sulk all she wants, but there was no need to get the police involved. She's overstepped the mark. She's probably afraid to come back now because she knows she's gone too far, grassing us up to the pigs.

The police interview was terrible. I wasn't ready for it, wasn't prepared for the questions. The two guys interviewing me were complete arseholes. I should have been more prepared. It's not like me. I thought about doing the whole 'no comment' thing that you see on the telly, but that would have made me look guilty so I tried to bluff my way through the whole thing. I kept tripping myself up. Nearly blurted out things I shouldn't.

Rachel better not come back after all this shit and act as if nothing's changed. She's putting me through all of this as a punishment – I know her and her silly moods. Well, she's out of the loop now – there's no way we can keep her involved after she's pulled this shit. No way. She's not going to get a penny now. It's her own fault. She can't be trusted.

The coppers still let me go. They had no reason to keep me and the two pigs were raging.

They kept asking me about my dad and Rachel. They spent ages trying to catch me out about it. They tried to say they were having an affair. Just like Laura had said. Just like they all had said. As if my dad would be so stupid. He wouldn't be so stupid. He better not have been so stupid.

The plan is well and truly screwed. There's no way we can get our hands on the money with this shit going on. It's not over – just on hold for the moment. Just until all this blows over.

61

Kat had been scouring the internet looking for any updates on the case for days now. She was refreshing various websites which dealt with the latest Glasgow news every two minutes or so. Rachel's details were on the Police Scotland website in the missing-person section. She also had the radio constantly on the local station, and she had the television locked on the news channel. She knew it was only a matter of time before something was announced. Things had gone annoyingly quiet since the melee in the park. All the news said was that Rachel was still missing. It had been an infuriating couple of days constantly refreshing the screen and she'd had precious little sleep over the weekend. This morning there was some news though. Kat listened intently to the hourly news report on the radio.

'Police have today arrested a 51-year-old man in connection with the disappearance of Glasgow woman Rachel Strang. Miss Strang has been missing for ten days now and police have confirmed today that they believe she has come to grievous harm and they are now treating the case as a murder enquiry. More on this breaking news when we get it…'

There it was. What Kat had been waiting for. She knew exactly who the 51-year-old man in question was. Her ex-husband Stephen. They must have found the phone! They must have seen the blood. Kat felt a tingle of excitement ripple through her. This was all her doing. She had set this in motion. It felt good knowing that Stephen would be getting his comeuppance – it was the least he deserved. The police had worked quickly. They knew that Rachel was dead and it was now a murder enquiry, though Kat had thought this would happen further down the line.

Stephen or 'Ste' had sent his daughter and stepdaughter into Kat's work and made her life a living hell, but it wasn't working out well for him now.

If the police were focusing their efforts on building a case on Stephen, or even looking at Jason, Tony or Kirsty for that matter, then they wouldn't be likely to come looking for Kat. In any case, why would they even class Kat as a suspect? The one thing she couldn't let herself become was complacent though. There was always a thought niggling away at her that she had missed something crucial. Something she had forgotten to wipe off the phone or some DNA evidence left behind. Some glaring error that would ruin everything and send her down for a long time.

Kat paced up and down the room. She knew the police would be going through the phone. They would be questioning Stephen about his affair with his stepdaughter. He would try to wriggle out of it, like he had done most of his life, but there was no way he could deny it had been going on. The amount of messages, along with the disgusting content was proof enough. The police could also look into it in more detail. They would be analysing phone calls between the two. It also looked terrible for Stephen that the phone had been found down the side of the couch in the small dingy shed in his garden. Hopefully the spots of blood had been found as well. Kat was sure they would be.

The case against him would be building quite nicely.

62

The call had come through early in the morning from a frantic member of the public. They'd stumbled upon a body whilst walking their dog in some woods. Immediately the Rachel Strang enquiry had been summoned.

Prentice and Donaldson had encountered numerous dead bodies in their time. Far too many. They'd seen horrible stuff. Donaldson had once seen a body that had lain in a flat up the Gallowgate for three months. It had stayed with him. The stench and the flies were something he would never forget. It had even made him miss lunch that day. Seeing Rachel Strang in that state would be up there though. It wasn't nice. Whoever had left her there had done a right number on her. She'd been burned and left to the elements, and it would take dental records to confirm with 100 per cent certainty that it was her, but unofficially the detectives had been told that the search was over and the murder enquiry could begin in earnest.

'They should hang that bastard for this,' Donaldson said.

'If it's him, then he'll never see the light of day again,' Prentice replied.

'Would you stop that? It's him. Everyone else can see it – why can't you?'

Prentice knew this was an argument he wasn't going to win. Seeing the girl's body like that meant they needed a result. Everyone did. There was no way whoever did this was going to get away with it. Nobody should be treated like that.

'Watch out, Al – that's the gaffer's here,' Donaldson said, indicating the arrival of their superior.

DCI Brannigan would be in front of the cameras imminently. This was his moment in the sun. He loved seeing himself on the telly, even if he usually made an arse of himself. There were rumours that he had DVDs of every television appearance he had ever made. Brannigan bundled his way out of a chauffeur-driven car and waded through the mud. He looked furious at the state of his shoes.

'Right, Alan. What have we found? Is it the young Strain girl?' Brannigan said.

'Strang her name is,' Prentice said. The least his boss could do was get her name right. 'But yes, sir, forensics tells us it looks like it's her. She's in a terrible state.'

'Well, let's get on with it and tell the press. Gather them round and we'll get the show on the road.' Brannigan was all heart – about as subtle as a brick to the face. He wanted in and out as quickly as possible; his statement to the press wouldn't exactly be heartfelt.

'Maybe best if we don't do it here, eh?' Prentice said. It was tactless to say the least to get in front of the cameras here. Plus, it was still an active crime scene.

Brannigan looked sternly at his inspector and reluctantly agreed.

63

Stephen Armstrong looked terrible. He looked even worse than the last time he had been interviewed. He now had two large purple-and-black bruises just under his eyes after the punch from Jason, days' worth of stubble and he looked like he hadn't slept a wink or had a meal since he'd been arrested. He was slumped forward in his chair with his head in his hands.

The formalities over once more, the interview commenced.

'Stephen. Why did you kill Rachel Strang?' Prentice started. There was no point beating about the bush.

'I didn't do this. I really didn't. You honestly have to believe me,' Stephen said.

'Why should we believe a single word that comes out of that lying mouth of yours?' Donaldson said.

'I never killed Rachel. I never killed her—'

'You were sleeping with her though – we've already established that. Although you denied that as well, didn't you? So why should we believe you now?' Donaldson asked. He was utterly convinced of Stephen's guilt. Stephen hadn't done himself any favours with his constant lies.

Stephen dragged his fingers through his greasy hair then spoke quietly. 'I didn't kill her.'

'Let's have a look at the evidence,' Donaldson began. 'Having an affair with your stepdaughter? Check. Incriminating phone calls, messages and photos? Check. DNA everywhere? Check. Rachel's phone found in *your* shed? Check. Rachel's blood found in your shed and on the couch? Check. You've got motive, means and opportunity.'

Donaldson was enjoying the interview. Stephen squirmed in his chair but didn't utter another word. He looked beaten. Defeated. He held his head in his hands and rocked slowly back and forth. Tears were not far away.

'What do you have to say for yourself, Stephen?' Prentice said.

'I never killed her,' Stephen said quietly.

'How did her blood end up in your shed?' Donaldson asked.

'I don't… I don't know. I never killed her,' Stephen said almost inaudibly.

'We've got Rachel's phone. It makes interesting reading,' Prentice told him. Stephen looked like he wanted the ground to open up and swallow him. 'There are a bundle of messages from you. There's loads of calls. There's photos. And there's this – an interesting little note written by Rachel herself. Let me read it for you:

'"It's getting too real now. Ste shouldn't be doing what he's doing with me. I'm scared to stop though – he's already threatened me and I think the next time he might go too far. I know his temper is real bad. I don't want to be on the end of it again. I'll need to try and get away. It's the only option. Ste will kill me otherwise. Kirsty as well. The two of them are a horrible pair. I wish they'd never come into my life."'

'What do you say to that, *Ste?*'

Stephen looked shocked. He grasped some of his greasy dank hair and pulled it as he continually rocked back and forth.

'I… never… killed her.'

'Okay, you say you never killed Rachel. Then who did?' Prentice asked.

'This is all wrong.' Stephen shook his head back and forth.

'Can you tell us why Rachel's blood is in your shed?' Donaldson asked.

'No. I can't believe this. It's all wrong,' Stephen said.

'Yes, Stephen, it is all wrong,' Prentice said. 'You've been having an affair with your stepdaughter, who has now been found murdered. And now we find spots of her blood in your shed, along with her phone. Plus, I'm sure once forensics are done there will be traces of you left on her body. You're going to have to do well to explain this away.'

Stephen and his lawyer sat in silence. They both knew this wasn't going well.

'There's no good explanation for any of this, is there, Stephen?' Prentice said. 'The only explanation is that you killed your stepdaughter. You killed Rachel, didn't you?'

'No,' he replied in a whisper. 'No. I never killed her.'

Donaldson brought out some photographs of Rachel's charred remains and spread them on the table. Numerous disgusting photographs.

'Look at her. You left her like that. You killed her and left her to rot in those woods. Look at her!' Donaldson shouted.

Stephen jerked forward and looked at the photographs for a brief moment. Sheer horror engulfed his face. He had gone an unhealthy shade of pale.

'Oh my God, I'm going to be sick,' he said.

64

'Miss Matthews?' Prentice said, flashing his warrant card, which hung around his neck from a lanyard. Kat opened the door further. 'I'm Detective Inspector Prentice and this is Detective Sergeant Donaldson. We'd like to talk to you about your ex-husband, a Mr Stephen Armstrong?'

'Stephen? I thought you'd be here about Rachel Strang,' Kat said. This was the moment of truth for her. She tried to remain calm.

'We are,' Prentice said. 'If we could maybe do this inside?'

There was no way Kat could get out of this. She opened the door and let the officers follow her inside.

Kat had thought she might get interviewed by the police again, especially when they found out Stephen was her ex-husband. The fact it was by two CID officers and not uniforms was worrying but not entirely unexpected – this was a murder enquiry after all.

The two detectives made for an odd couple. They took a seat on the couch where Rachel had sat just a few weeks before. Kat tried to put that thought out of her mind.

'When was the last time you saw your ex-husband?' Prentice said.

'Thankfully not for a long time. You said you were here about Stephen and Rachel – what's going on?' Kat said. She had remained composed so far.

'We believe Stephen was having an affair with Miss Strang, and we believe he may have something to do with her death,' Donaldson said.

'What? Stephen and Rachel?'

'Let me explain,' Prentice said. 'Your ex-husband is married again, to a lady called Laura Strang—'

'Strang?'

'Yes, Strang,' said Prentice. 'Rachel was Laura's daughter, and we now know that he was having an affair with his stepdaughter.'

Kat tried to appear shocked.

'I know this is a lot to take in,' Donaldson said.

'You're telling me. You mean I work in the same place as my ex-husband's stepdaughter and they were—'

'Yes. That appears to be the case. We're gathering as much information about Stephen as possible. We think he is heavily involved in all of this. We've been going around his friends and acquaintances and your name popped up in our enquiries. I know you've been divorced for a long time, but is there anything you could tell us about him that might help?' Prentice said.

'I can't believe this. Stephen was a lot of things but a murderer? I don't know. I can tell you one thing though – it doesn't surprise me that he was having an affair. That's the reason I left him. He liked younger women. I caught him in the act one time and the girl was lucky if she was old enough.'

The two detectives sat opposite Kat shared a look.

'I know you've not been together for a good while but do you know of any places Stephen liked to go or take anyone?' Prentice asked.

'You wouldn't exactly call Stephen a romantic,' Kat said. 'We never went anywhere – we never went on holiday; we barely went out for a meal. One time he took me to some bloody woods—'

'Woods?' Donaldson said. 'Where were these woods?' Both Prentice and Donaldson had moved to the edge of their seats. Their interest was most definitely piqued.

'Not too far outside Glasgow; I'm not exactly sure where. I just remember it was a grubby, derelict place. We pitched a tent and everything,' Kat said. She knew the officers were interested. 'What is it? What have I said?'

Donaldson looked at Prentice – Prentice nodded as if giving his partner the go-ahead to say what he was thinking.

'This information hasn't been released yet,' Donaldson said. 'We found

Rachel's body in woods just outside Glasgow this morning.'

'Oh my God. Stephen did this, didn't he?' Kat didn't have to fake her shock this time. Rachel's body had been found. Kat hadn't thought for one minute the body would be found so quickly. It was foolish thinking, as there were probably hundreds of police officers and members of the public looking for her. Plus, the media interest was high. It didn't change anything though. There was a slim chance Kat's DNA could be on the body, but after over a month it was unlikely. Over a month in which there had been near torrential rain. A month in which the body would have been left to the elements and whatever wildlife was in that area. This after all the bleach, the white spirit and the fire had ravaged her body. Kat shuddered to think what state the body would be in.

'We obviously can't say for sure but it's looking like Mr Armstrong was involved,' Prentice said. Donaldson would have been far more forthright in his answer. Kat tried to stop herself from smiling. This was all going according to plan.

*

If Prentice was looking for any inkling that Stephen Armstrong might not be their man, he wasn't going to find it here. His ex-wife hadn't exactly given him a glowing character reference. Maybe he was wrong after all? Maybe he was seeing things that weren't really there. Niggling doubts always existed in cases like these, and even Prentice had to admit that everything he had uncovered so far pointed to Stephen Armstrong being their killer.

65

DCI Brannigan had called the meeting, but his chair remained empty. He was late, as usual. Rumours around the room were that the DCI was caught up watching reruns of himself on the news. The detectives spoke about the case amongst themselves whilst awaiting his arrival.

'It's the stepdad,' Donaldson said, biting into a sausage and bacon sandwich.

'It's not looking good for him, I'll give you that, but we still need to keep an open mind,' Prentice replied.

'Stepdad,' Donaldson said with his mouth full. He wasn't one to abandon his opinions. He was adamant, and even Prentice had to admit he was probably right. The evidence certainly pointed that way.

'What about the boyfriend?' Prentice offered.

'He's got a temper – we saw that when he was arrested,' DS Kelly said. 'But murdering his fiancée? That's a stretch. Plus, he seems genuinely too clueless to get away with it.'

'I'm telling you, Al, it's the stepdad. It's absolutely ripping out of him. Plus the evidence is there for all to see,' Donaldson said, savouring another mouthful of his roll. Donaldson loved to eat but breakfast seemed to be his favourite meal of the day. Prentice had never seen someone consume so many calories in the morning.

'I'm not saying he's not a good suspect, and the evidence against him is mounting up, but I just think we need to look a bit deeper.'

'Why waste our time looking at someone else?' Donaldson said. 'We've got our man. I'm sure of it. I can feel it in my water. Plus, he's been helped by that daughter of his.'

Prentice knew he'd have his work cut out trying to convince his friend – and the rest of the team for that matter – to look at some of the other suspects. The evidence had stacked up against the stepdad, Stephen Armstrong. He'd admitted having an inappropriate relationship with Rachel, and he'd admitted sending the texts found on her phone, but he still wasn't copping to the murder. The forensic evidence against him was the real clincher though. There was no plausible explanation for Rachel's blood ending up all over his shed. Something niggled at Prentice though – it was just… it was just all a bit too easy. The text and the subsequent meeting had laid out the suspects on a plate for them and Prentice didn't like the fact the text had been anonymous.

The problem with Stephen Armstrong – and the reason Donaldson, Kelly and the other detectives were adamant he was the guilty man – was that he'd lied. He'd lied through his teeth about everything and only later, when presented with irrefutable evidence, had he held his hands up. Prentice couldn't be sure what was truth and what were lies when it came to the answers he gave.

The door opened and DCI Brannigan breezed in without so much as an apology for his tardiness. He took his seat and looked at his squad of detectives.

'Morning, folks,' Brannigan began. 'Short but sweet meeting this morning. I've just come from a meeting and basically the gist of it is – we've got him. It would have been good if Archie Thomson was involved somehow, but we can't have everything now, can we? Sterling work from everyone. Absolutely first-class effort. The forensic evidence added to the rest of it means that this guy Armstrong hasn't got a leg to stand on. We've got enough. We're going to charge him with the murder of his stepdaughter.'

66

Working at the bank had changed completely over the past few weeks. Not only for Kat but for everyone in the office. Rachel's disappearance had meant nothing was ever going to be the same again.

Kat was allowed to go about her business without fear of any bullying. Rachel was gone, never to return and Kirsty hadn't been seen since the police took her away at the park. No one was sure what was going on with her – or if she was even still employed by the company. This suited Kat down to the ground. She didn't want to see her back.

Kat had been given an interview for the manager's position, along with four other candidates, last week. It had gone really well and she was just waiting to hear if she had been successful. She had prepared thoroughly for it and had even bought herself a new trouser suit. It looked like the one the female detective had worn when she'd interviewed Kat about Rachel. She'd answered all the questions well and there had been no awkward silences. She had come across as confident and assured. She had even highlighted her loyalty to the company and asked a few questions of her own, which the interview panel had seemed genuinely pleased with.

Tony was leaving at the end of the month, but he had already completely given up on the role. He had hardly come out of his office since Rachel's disappearance had blown up spectacularly, though when he did he looked terrible and always as if he had been crying. He had been questioned thoroughly by the police several times now, thanks in part to Kat pointing out how upset he was.

Everyone in the office had exhausted all questions and speculation as to what had actually happened to Rachel. Every day now, everyone in the office listened to the news on the hour, every hour to see if there were any updates on the case, though there had been precious few updates since Stephen had been charged. However, today was different. Today there was news. Big news.

Everyone in the office was silent as they listened to the news report.

'Police have today confirmed remains found in woodland near Glasgow are those of missing woman Rachel Strang. The nineteen-year-old has been missing since...'

The news came out of the blue for everyone in the office, apart from Kat. The place was buzzing with chatter now. Nearly everyone had assumed that Rachel was dead, but it was still a shock for them to have it confirmed. A few of the girls were in tears. Any hopes people had about her being found alive had been extinguished. Kat had to play along and show she was as shocked as the rest of them.

Everyone turned to the office where Tony was in hiding. There was a horrible animal-like noise. Tony was wailing loudly – his worst fears had been realised.

67

It's all gone wrong.

I can't believe this.

Rachel's dead.

Dead.

And the police are trying to blame me and my dad.

I've been questioned three or four times now and I can tell they don't believe me, even though I'm telling the truth. I never killed anyone. I never had anything to do with Rachel dying. It's like a living nightmare.

They'll not let me see Dad. I'm not sure I even want to see him at the moment. The detective, Prentice, showed me things that confirm he was having a relationship with Rachel. Messages between the two of them. Photos they sent each other. Photos! I feel so humiliated. Why would he jeopardise everything for her? Why couldn't he just leave her alone? Stupid. So stupid.

He would never kill her though. No chance. There's no way he would do anything like that – I know that for a fact. There's just no way. No matter how often they keep asking me. There's no way my dad's a murderer.

I think the police are going to actually charge him. With murder. Fucking hell. It's unreal. I can tell they think I knew something or I helped in some way. How could he be so stupid to have an affair with her? He's ruined everything. And then he lied to my face about it. What else could he be lying about? All that shit about Fat Kat being my mum and abandoning me –I'm beginning to think it's all lies. Especially when she kept her son. Why would she do that? None of it makes sense anymore. It's an actual living nightmare all of this.

I don't know what we're going to do. What I'm going to do. I really don't. It's all gone to shit.

68

There seemed to be every newspaper for sale that day floating around the office. Tabloids and broadsheets. Every last morsel of news on the case had been digested. Every news website had been read and reread. Refreshed and refreshed some more. The radio was on constantly. No one wanted to miss any developments in the case. There wasn't much work being done but nobody seemed to care.

Tony hadn't appeared at work this morning, and it was left to a manager in another department to announce that a counsellor was on site should anyone feel the need to see them. On the whole though, people were being left to their own devices.

*

The work day was nearly at an end when the email appeared in Kat's inbox. She had been eagerly awaiting its arrival since her interview. It stared at her.

Application for Team Manager Role

Kat's heart was pounding. She was filled with a mix of excitement and trepidation. She had prepared thoroughly for the interview and knew it had gone well, but there were doubts in the back of her mind – there were always doubts, though not as many as before. If she didn't get it, was it really the end of the world? Of course not – it showed how far she'd come that she had actually applied for the job in the first place.

Kat had been passed over for promotion years ago and had never applied for another step up since. She had actually gone the other way and been demoted, as the strain of being a single parent and looking after a young boy had impacted her work, and she'd had to just scrape by as her wages decreased – Stephen wasn't interested in seeing Paul and hadn't paid one penny towards his upbringing, which was all the more galling after the revelation that he had a daughter of his own. It had been hard. It had been a struggle, but she had managed to get through it. The bullying had killed her already broken confidence but now that too was at an end.

And she had gathered up the courage and applied for the manager's job to be vacated by Terrible Tony.

She clicked open the email.

Congratulations, we would like to offer you the position...

Kat had done it. As she sat reading the email, her heart still pounding, a small tear fell from her eye. Not a tear of sadness – it was joy. She was so proud of herself, and she hadn't had that feeling since she was a small girl. For years the life had been sucked from her by a no-good husband, doubters and bullies, people telling her she was no good, she was too fat, too ugly – the list was endless. All of the hurtful comments had dragged her down and taken away every ounce of confidence she had ever had. She had been through so much since the incident with Rachel. She hadn't meant for it to happen, but it had and there was nothing she could do about that now. She couldn't magically go back and undo any of it.

Reading the email, she realised that all these negative feelings had evaporated. Who cared that she was in her fifties now? She believed her life was restarting, she was energised again and she felt great. She felt alive.

69

Brannigan and the rest of the top brass were more than happy to charge Stephen Armstrong. Prentice had to admit that the evidence was good and went far beyond circumstantial. They had listened to him cast doubts on the whole case against Stephen but everyone was quite content that they'd get a result. Prentice was sure they'd get a conviction too. The CPS was also convinced. There was still something niggling away at Prentice though.

Stephen and his daughter Kirsty had a strange relationship, to say the least, and their behaviour had been puzzling, but were they capable of what happened to Rachel? Maybe it was an accident that had spiralled out of control. Prentice didn't know. He still had doubts, but he seemed to be the only one. In fact, he knew he was the only one.

The thing that didn't sit right with him about all of this was the text. Who had sent all of the texts to everyone and to the police? Who had arranged for them all to be there at that specific location and time? Brannigan and the rest of the detectives wanted Prentice to leave it alone. They said he shouldn't look a gift horse in the mouth, but it felt strange. They'd had tip-offs before, of course, but to his knowledge they'd never had all the suspects in a case delivered to them on a platter like that. It was just too easy.

The rest of the team were quite happy with the outcome. Prentice could hear the whispers every time he entered a room – there's the guy who wanted to blow this result for them. The whole case had been wrapped up quickly, far quicker than the majority Prentice had worked on. Stephen Armstrong and his daughter Kirsty would likely be jailed for a considerable period of time.

He would enjoy seeing the sister being told she was being charged for helping her dad get rid of the body and covering up the murder. She seemed like she didn't have a care in the world. It would be a pleasure wiping the smile off her face.

70

'Police have today charged 51-year-old Stephen Armstrong with the murder of his nineteen-year-old stepdaughter Rachel Strang. Glasgow girl Rachel had been missing for five weeks until a member of the public found a body in woodland near Glasgow yesterday. Kirsty Armstrong, Stephen Armstrong's daughter has also been charged in relation to the case, although her role is, as yet, unknown. It has emerged that stepfather Armstrong and Miss Strang were involved in an affair, though a police spokesman refused to confirm or deny these allegations. More on this as we get it.'

Kat didn't know how to feel. Everything had worked out exactly how she had wanted. Her plan had come to fruition and then some. Yet she felt a bit numb. Lives had been ruined because of the events which had spiralled from Rachel's accidental death in the car park. Rachel was dead. Stephen would likely spend the rest of his days behind bars. Kirsty would probably spend time in jail as well. Rachel's mother had lost her daughter and had her marriage ripped apart. No one had come out of this well. No one apart from Kat that is.

It was on every news bulletin on the hour, every hour. Speculation was rife and some of the tabloids were embellishing the story even further. It seemed a stepdad sleeping with and then killing his stepdaughter with help from his biological daughter wasn't sensational enough for them. The papers had managed to get hold of photos showing Stephen, Kirsty, Rachel and various other family members. It was surreal seeing the whole thing in print and online.

The headlines were numerous: 'Stepdad charged with murder', 'Gruesome dad and daughter killed Rachel', 'Horror family killing' and (Kat's personal favourite) 'Twisted stepdad and daughter abused and killed Rachel'.

Kat was going to be late for work at this rate. She had been up since the crack of dawn digesting every last morsel of news on the case. She tried to dig deeper than most would – she tried to get a sense of what the police were saying or what evidence they had; tried to get a sense of what the police weren't saying as well. Not one news item suggested that any other suspects were being sought in relation to the case. Kat didn't want to admit it to herself, but it was looking good. It was all going according to plan. She had dealt with the questions from the two CID officers well and it looked like no suspicion would be laid upon her.

Kat put her earphones in and left the house. She wasn't going to work by car or by underground this morning.

She was walking it.

71

'Did you know? You knew, didn't you?'

'Hi, Mum. Knew what?' Kat smiled. Maureen, for once, wasn't seated in her usual chair watching television. She was excitedly pacing up and down the room. She had been waiting for her daughter's visit all day.

'Don't start all that coy nonsense with me. You know fine well what I'm talking about. You're ex-bloody-husband and that little cow.'

'I know as much as you do, Mum. I read it in the papers like everyone else,' Kat said, indicating the large pile of well-thumbed newspapers on the coffee table which her mother had been reading and rereading.

'Aye, so you did.' Maureen smiled at Kat. 'So you bloody did. Take a seat and tell me everything. And I mean everything.'

*

Kat parked her new car further down the street. The Mercedes was in her space yet again. Some things never changed it seemed.

She got out of the brand-new Mini and walked to her flat. She wasn't the least bit annoyed. In fact, she couldn't hide the smile on her face.

The young man with the flash suit was standing staring at his car. He had his mobile phone clamped to his ear as usual but today he looked absolutely furious.

'This was you, wasn't it?' he said as Kat approached.

'What are you talking about?' Kat said.

'My car... it was you!'

Kat took a look at the damage. Somebody had put a half brick through the driver's-side window and there was a large score on the paintwork.

'Fuck off,' Kat said, laughing as she walked away.

Acknowledgements

Firstly, thank you to everyone who has bought the book, I really appreciate it and hope you enjoyed it.

Thanks to my wife Tricia for all of her encouragement and to my four year old Aaron for scribbling over the various drafts with pictures of dinosaurs.

Thanks to ex policeman and all round good guy William Davey for his help and knowledge. I owe you a drink.

Thanks to my editor Laura Kincaid who helped greatly.

Thanks to my cover design team at BooksCovered, especially Stuart Bache and Emily. Love your work.

Thanks also to Mark Dawson, James Blatch and the team at SPF for helping me on the road to writing.

A special thanks to my wonderful mum and dad who have always supported me.

Thanks again,
Ewan

Printed in Great Britain
by Amazon